HARD MEN RIDING

Texan man Raynor, and his Mexican compadre Santos, had once been in Jake Petch's gang of bank robbers. After a raid in Grantsburg, Petch had bushwhacked Raynor and Santos, left them for dead and taken all the gold. Two years later, Raynor learns that Petch is now a big rancher in Arizona, and sets out with Santos on the vengeance trail. They leave a long tally of dead men before they finally face Petch. Can they settle the score?

ELLIOT CONWAY

HARD MEN RIDING

Complete and Unabridged

LINFORD
Leicester

First published in Great Britain in 2007 by
Robert Hale Limited
London

First Linford Edition
published 2008
by arrangement with
Robert Hale Limited
London

British Library CIP Data

Conway, Elliot
    Hard men riding.—Large print ed.—
Linford western library
    1. Western stories
    2. Large type books
    I. Title
    823.9'14 [F]

ISBN 978–1–84782–164–5

Published by
F. A. Thorpe (Publishing)
Anstey, Leicestershire

Set by Words & Graphics Ltd.
Anstey, Leicestershire
Printed and bound in Great Britain by
T. J. International Ltd., Padstow, Cornwall

This book is printed on acid-free paper

*For Ron Newton and his good lady
wife, Joyce, in remembrance
of when the dawn came up
like thunder.*

PROLOGUE

Jake Petch, a heavily built, hard-faced man, whose brutal looks were emphasized by an old knife scar that ran from his right ear to the point of his chin, gave a grunt of satisfaction as he saw the last of his gang ride into town. It was time to do what they had ridden into Grantsburg for: to take the gold from the safe of the First National Bank. Petch eased his pistol in its sheath before stepping down from the saloon porch and walking across the street to the bank.

Petch hadn't picked the Grantsburg bank to rob out of his hat; he'd had information that two days ago the Eastern cattle buyers attending a big cattle sale had deposited a strong-box full of gold coins in the bank, brought here by a specially hired Butterfield stage with an escort of six heavily

1

armed men. The Yankees may have whupped the South during the war, but that didn't mean the Texas ranchers were willing to accept Yankee greenbacks for their longhorns: they were demanding gold coins in settlement of their deals.

Petch saw that Main Street was still quiet. It would be like taking candy from a store. He also had another plan, one that would give him all the bank's gold. Petch wanted to be rich enough to quit the bank and stage-heisting business so that he could set himself up as a big rancher and saloon owner. A five-way split of the bank's takings wouldn't get him far along the road to being a big man in Arizona. His future ambitions needed all the gold to make them a reality.

He had sounded out Seth Hardropp, the gang member he thought would put the promise of getting a half share of the pot before his loyalty to the other three members of the gang. Petch gave a ghost of a smile. And that would be all the son-of-a-bitch would get, a promise, and a bullet in his back after he had helped to put paid to Raynor, his Mexican partner, and old man Baxter.

Hardropp had given him a suspicious-eyed, calculating look when he had suggested the plan to him.

'It'll mean killin' the other three,' he said, 'Or they'll hunt for us as long as it takes and gun us down for double-crossin' them.'

Petch wolf-grinned. 'I'd taken that into consideration, Seth, That's why I need you as a partner. I couldn't take the three of them on my own. Ain't no man I know can bring out a gun and kill with it faster than Raynor. And Santos ain't that much slower. Are you in or out then?' If Hardropp cried chicken then the bank raid might have to be called off because he would be a man short. He would have to shoot Hardropp in case he blabbed to the other three about the deal he had been offered, or he would get dead. But he

3

needn't have worried: he could see the greed showing in Hardropp's eyes.

'A half cut rests easier with me than a fifth does, Petch,' Hardropp said. 'I'm in.'

The raid couldn't have gone off any smoother than it did. The four cocked pistols and a double-barrelled shotgun wielded by men with dead-or-alive wanted flyers out on them, quickly convinced the bank manager that if he refused to open up his safe he would be responsible not only for his own painful demise but that of three members of his staff and two elderly customers. And he quickly opined that all the gold in Fort Knox, let alone in his bank, wasn't worth shedding all that innocent blood.

'Open the safe,' he told his chief teller.

As usual after a raid, the gang, once clear of the town, split up so as not to leave bold wide horse tracks for the posses that would be raised behind them to follow. After this raid they were to meet up after dark to share out the gold at a deserted barn at the mouth of Sawmill Creek, a rendezvous chosen by Petch as being well clear of the main trails, and where men could be killed without the shooting raising any fuss.

As dusk was closing in, Raynor, riding along the narrow creek-side trail met up with José Santos, his *amigo*. The pair had worked together as road agents long before joining Petch's gang. Nearing the barn, Jud Baxter came out of the brush and joined them. All congratulated themselves on how easy the raid had been, all eager to get their cut of the takings to spend on several months of high living in the saloons and cathouses of the Panhandle. The sudden burst of rifle fire bloodily ended the trio's good time thoughts.

Petch and Hardropp came down from the ridge, warily, rifles ready to pull off a finishing shot, to check out their deadly handiwork.

'Old Baxter's here, Petch!' Hardropp called out. 'He's a goner! I can't see any

5

sign of Raynor or his greaser buddy though!'

'Don't fret any, Seth,' replied Petch. 'They'll be floatin' down the crick. The amount of shells we fired would've wiped out a whole troop of cavalry. Have a look along the edge of the crick to see if their bodies are trapped in the weeds close by.'

Hardropp walked to the water's edge and bent down to have a closer look at the dark, fast-running water. He didn't hear the shot that killed him, just felt a searing flash of pain then complete darkness. His body splashed into the creek and Petch, as he loaded his pistol, watched it disappear from his sight.

He grinned for real as he walked back to his horse. It had been one hell of a good day, he thought. And someone else would hit a good streak, unexpectedly: the man who came along the trail and found four riderless horses, and all their gear, standing there just for the taking.

Petch mounted up and rode west out

of Texas to where no lawmen held papers on Jake Petch, bank robber, to start up his new life as bona-fide cattle rancher and to make it big where he finally swung down from his horse.

1

It was barely first light when the lone rider splashed his way across the shallows of the Rio Bravo. Once clear of the river the gringos called the Rio Grande, the rider cut away from the Mexican border village of El Parvene and headed south-west with some speed across the stony acrid badlands of northern Sonora towards the dark mass of the Sierras, the sawtoothed ridges of which were silhouetted against the far horizon.

The rider, a gringo, sat tall in the saddle, as lean-framed as his high-stepping, ground-eating mount with a face as hard-looking as the land he was riding over. He was a man who favoured wearing two pistols. The butts of the twin .44 Walker Colts, sheathed in holsters belted about his middle, were facing outwards in the style of a cross draw *pistolero*. The seven-load Spencer carbine, held easy across his saddlehorn, had a .45 shell levered in its firing chamber. He was what the old mountain men called, loaded for bear.

The rider hadn't been in Mexico before but he knew that like the border territory north of the Rio Grande, it would be a land where broncos, red and brown, would use it as their own stomping ground, to kill, maim, and rob any lone traveller at their will.

As he reached the rising foothills of the mountains, he saw a huddle of flat-roofed buildings. 'Horse,' he said, 'that place up ahead, if I've followed the trail right, is Casa Grande. Grand Castles.' He snorted. 'These Mexes sure pick fancy names for their dog-dirt habitations.'

Ten minutes later he was drawing up his horse in the middle of the village, in the noonday heat deserted except for a man wrapped up in his serape sitting with his back against the shaded wall of the largest building in the village, and a young boy drawing water from a high-walled well. The gringo heeled his horse over to the boy.

'*Buenos dias, chico*,' he said. 'I'm takin' that this place is Casa Grande. If it is, does Señor Santos still live here?'

The boy spun round in surprise, almost dropping the bucket of water he had hauled up from the well. He hadn't seen many gringos before and certainly not one as tall and riding a fine horse. He had to crane his neck to look the gringo in the eyes, which were as hard-looking as the stones he was standing on.

'*Sí* this is Casa Grande, *señor*,' he replied. 'And the *hombre* you ask for, is it Señor José Santos, the fierce *bandido*?'

The rider sighed. He hadn't hard-assed all this way south for damn all.

'That's the fella, boy,' he said, and grinned down at him. 'I heard tell he was once a *mal hombre*, a fierce *pistolero*. He's still here then?'

The boy nodded. '*Sí, señor*, that's his

house next to the cantina.' He pointed to a small pock-marked adobe building next to the one where the sleeping man lay.

'*Bueno*,' the gringo said, as he swung down from his saddle. He handed the boy a silver coin. '*Amigo*,' he said, 'I would be obliged if you'd give my horse a pail of that sweet water you're drawin', then lead him somewhere outa this goddamned heat and ease the saddle straps, *comprende*?'

The boy gave the tall gringo a flashing, white-toothed smile as he fingered the coin. '*Comprende, señor*,' he said. 'And I will also brush down your fine Yankee horse.' He grabbed hold of the reins and, with a bucket of water held in his other hand, led the horse towards the rear of the cantina.

Still holding the Spencer, old self-preservation habits never dying away, the gringo, John Raynor strode across to the home of his former *compadre*, his owlhoot partner, José Santos. A man whom he had dragged, shot several times, from Sawmill Creek over two years ago. Raynor's face steeled over as memories of that grim night returned.

The pair of them had been riding along Sawmill Creek trail, joined along the way by Jud Baxter to meet up with Petch and Hardropp at the old barn for the sharing out of the gold. He had caught a glimpse of a look on Petch's face as they split up outside Grantsburg that had unsettled him. He was remembering that look now as he scanned the tree-covered ridge to their left. It was too dark to see any movement, but he knew there was danger for them up there on the high ground. The feeling was strong enough for him to alert José and Jud.

'Boys,' he said, 'I'm gettin' a bad feelin' ridin' along here in the dark. Or I'm gettin' the nerves of an old maid. But Petch gave me a look before he rode off as though he was seein' me for the last time. Once I get my share of the gold I'm quittin' the gang. If you're havin' doubts about your boss what the hell else is there to do?'

Before the other two could comment on his fears all hell broke loose in a non-stop blaze of rifle fire.

He flung himself out of his saddle and rolled down the low bank, conscious of two burning pains in his left side as he hit the water. He struggled up on to his feet in the chest high icy water then felt something bump against him. In spite of being shot he could still worry that 'gators could live in the creek. That frightening thought only lasted a second or two because he had never heard that 'gators groaned. He reached out and grabbed José Santos before he was washed away downstream and lifted his head clear of the water, grimly noting, by the stickiness of blood on his fingers, that his *compadre* had been badly wounded. He dragged his body deeper into the thick belt of reeds as he heard voices at the edge of the creek: Petch and Hardropp's, their former partners' voices. He cursed softly but profanely.

A few tense, painful seconds later, his wounds stinging like animal bites, Raynor heard the sound of a single shot then the loud splash of something heavy falling into the creek. A dark shape swirled past him and he reckoned that Seth Hardropp had paid the price of trusting Petch in whatever deal Petch had offered him. It would be one less son-of-a-bitch to kill when he was fit enough to get on the trail of Petch.

After a short while he heard the sound of a horse riding away and only then did he clamber out of the creek. Hauling Santos on to dry land took all the strength he still had left. Only the cold, vengeful thoughts that some day he would face Petch and make him pay the full price for his treachery kept him going. He heaved Santos across his horse, then groaning with the effort, got into his saddle. As he rode out he looked over his shoulder into the blackness behind him. 'Jud,' he said. 'You're lyin' out there dead somewhere, but I promise you this, old-timer, when

I catch up with Petch one of the shells I'll put into his dirty hide will be for you.'

★ ★ ★

It took several minutes before a tequila brain-fuddled José Santos figured out that someone was hammering on his front door. He opened one blood-shot eye and growled out curses loud enough, he hoped, for whoever it was at the door to hear and *vamoose* and allow him to sleep off his night's heavy drinking session.

The knocking still persisted forcing Santos to fling off the dirty blanket that covered him and roll off his cot and get unsteadily to his feet. Santos, a squat built man, hitched up his pants over his sagging gut and padded barefoot to the door, a long-barrelled pistol held in his right hand all set to bounce it off the head of the son-of-a-bitch who had disturbed his sleep.

He pulled open the door, the brilliant

15

sunlight making him squint, so he could only see the vague outline of the man who was standing there. He knew the man was too tall to be a villager, and that fact stayed his pistol-whipping hand for a moment.

'Jesus, *compadre*!' he heard a gringo voice say. 'You looked better that night I dragged you outa that crick, José!'

Santos rocked back on his heels, eyes blinking in astonishment. As well as not being able to walk steady, was he that drunk he was hearing ghost voices from the past, he wondered? Then full vision came into his eyes and he saw clearly the tall, long-faced gringo standing there.

'*Madre de Dios*!' he gasped. 'Juan! I thought you would have been shot or hanged by the Texas Rangers by now. Have you come to my village to escape those man-huntin' sonsuvbitches?'

'No I haven't, *amigo*,' Raynor replied. 'And I ain't hard-assed all the way down from the Nations just to gaze on the ugly face of the fierce *bandido*, José

Santos.' He grinned. 'That's what the kid at the well called you.' Hard-faced again, he added, 'I came to tell you that I know where Petch is. I thought that you'd want to ride with me to settle up with the bush-whackin' bastard.'

Raynor knew that his former partner was an ugly-faced *hombre* but the expression of hatred he was showing now as he spat out a string of curses on Petch, his mother and grandmother's heads, would have scared the breech clout off a warpainted Apache bronco.

'Come inside, *amigo*,' Santos said after he had run out of curses. 'And we will talk about how we are goin' to kill that pig, Petch. But first you must tell me how you fared after you left me at Señor Barker's.'

Raynor sat down on the only chair in the room, a loose-legged piece of furniture. Santos sat on the edge of his cot and took a swallow from a bottle of tequila standing on the dirt floor at the head of the bed. He offered the bottle to Raynor.

17

Raynor grinned and shook his head. 'Not for me, pard. I haven't had a regular meal since I don't know when. A coupla of pulls at the bottle of fire-water and I'd pass out till sundown.' He took a quick glance around the 'fearsome' *bandido*'s room. It looked as homely as a pig pen and smelt no sweeter. Like him, Santos hadn't been living high on the hog since Petch had taken their share of the gold.

'I managed to get you to old Doc Barker,' he began. 'Knowin' that he patches up gunshot wounds without askin' a fella how he came by them. I didn't know whether you were dead or still breathin', bein' I was kinda passing out every now and again on the way. My wounds were hurtin' like hell, but the doc told me that they were through wounds and only wanted cleaning up to stop them from goin' bad on me. You were knockin' at the Pearly Gates.' Raynor smiled. 'And dirty-mouthin' something awful to listen to. Knowing that there'd be a big hunt set up for us in Grantsburg, I didn't want the doc to explain why he had two gunshot-wounded, suspicious-lookin' characters on his premises so I rode out, headin' for the Nations. And at a mighty slow pace I'll tell you. Four or five months later I happened to swing by Doc Barker's place to see if you had pulled through OK. He told me that you were fine considerin' all that lead Petch had put in you, plus the unexpected bath in the crick, and that you had lit out for Mexico. So I rode back to the Nations and joined up with a bunch of hard men who were holed up at a ranch of sorts called Younger's Bend.' Raynor gave a twist of a smile. 'I made enough to get by providin' I didn't eat too regularly and kept out of the cathouses and bars. Then two weeks ago a fella showed up and in general conversation he told me and the boys that he had met up with this fella Petch. Petch had once robbed banks with him, in someplace in Arizona and had made a name for himself, big rancher, saloon owner and suchlike. Though he now calls himself Jackson Pearson. This fella described Petch real well even to the knife scar on the sonuvabitch's face. So here I am, *amigo*, ready to hit the trail to Gila Crossing, Arizona, and settle up with Petch. I figured you'd want to ride with me, José.'

He looked at Santos thinking that in the state he was in, his old *compadre* would be hard pressed to ride to the edge of the village without falling out of his saddle.

Santos didn't answer him. He just sat there having his own thoughts about the night of the shooting and lying on Doc Barker's bed hovering between life and death and surprising the doc by staying alive. He had left long before he was fit enough to attempt the long ride back to Casa Grande but it wasn't in his nature to accept any more charity from Doc Barker than he had already had. Yet the doc had told him not to worry about the bill he owed.

'Raynor told me how Petch had

double-crossed you both,' Doc Barker had said. 'So if you get back your share of the gold you can pay me what you owe me. Now go easy on the ride back to Sonora, or you'll open up your wounds and there's no Raynor to bring you back here again. That tall gringo saved your life.'

Although he was a man who had committed most of the sins in the book Santos believed that the Holy *Madre* must have smiled down on him on the long ride south, or he would have ended up as a pile of bones somewhere along the trail. Only to end up as the village drunkard, he thought bitterly. If the hated Petch walked suddenly through his doorway he lacked the steadiness of a pistol hand to gun him down.

He looked at Raynor, face showing some firmness. '*Amigo*,' he said, 'you can see that I am not the *hombre* you once rode with, but if you're willin' to give me a few hours I will be able to ride with you to Arizona and spit in

Petch's face before we kill him. That's if you still want me as your *compadre*.'

'*Amigo*,' Raynor replied, 'I've been waiting since that night we finished up in that goddamned creek to gun down Petch; a few more hours waitin' won't upset me any. You sort yourself out. I'll go across to the cantina and have something to eat and rest up a spell. He grinned at Santos. 'Right now, pard, I sure don't feel like a fearsome desperado myself.'

★   ★   ★

It was well past noon when the cantina owner shook the tall gringo lying on his cot in the back room awake.

'*Señor*,' he said, 'Santos has sent word that he is ready to ride out.' Then stood back sharply from the cot. If the gringo *pistolero* once rode with the blood-thirsty *bandido*, José Santos, then he could have the same evil temper when aroused from sleeping and shoot his cantina to pieces with his

22

big pistols. To his relief the gringo did not show such wild traits as he got off the cot. Instead, he only asked for a bowl of water to freshen himself up with. Then he asked if he wanted payment for the use of his cot.

'Nada,' the cantina owner said, anxious to have the gringo *mal hombre* out of his cantina, and away from his village.

Raynor swilled water over his face, dried himself off then buckled on his gunbelt. Picking up the Spencer he stepped out into the open. Santos was already mounted and the Mexican boy was standing rein-holding his horse ready for him to do likewise. Santos, he noticed, had put on a serape and cleaner pants and was wearing his saw-toothed spurred boots, and was armed for war, He had a big pistol stuck down the top of his pants, a machete hanging at his right hip and held a rifle across his saddlehorn. In true *bandido* style the pistol and rifle reloads were held in a bandolier slung across his chest. More satisfying to Raynor, his partner had the hard-eyed gaze of the *pistolero* he had been in their heisting days. He had no doubts now that Santos would make the long trip to Arizona even if it meant crawling the last few miles.

The boy watched them ride out with wide-eyed awe. He had only heard tell that José Santos had been a much wanted *bandido* who robbed gringo banks, but he had only seen him as a dirty, regularly drunk old man. Now that Santos was savage-faced, loaded with weapons, the boy knew he was seeing him the way the gringos he robbed must have seen him.

A real *mal hombre*, a bad man. Though the tall gringo didn't look as fierce, the boy knew that he would also be an *hombre* much feared.

2

Petch, jaybird naked underneath his fancy patterned silk robe, was standing on the balcony of Gila Crossing's sporting house, cooling off after a heavy session with Señora Elizabeta, the raven-haired Mexican widow, who bossed over the string of short-time girls who serviced the sporting-house's many customers. Two years of good living had fleshed out Petch's face and waist somewhat. When dressed in one of his Eastern tailored suits, a white shirt with frilled cuffs and hand-tooled, soft leather boots — he had even hidden his facial scar by favouring wide sideburns — it would have taken someone who knew him real well in his old days to recognize him as Petch the bank robber.

Petch had not only changed his appearance but his name. He was known to the town's business community as Mr Jackson Pearson, hailing from Lothro Springs, Nevada, where, he had casually let drop, he owned a silver mine with a mother lode so rich running through it that an Eastern mining concern had bought him out, cash on the barrel head, and at his price. He was making the gold stolen from the Grantsburg bank work. He had bought a dead colonel's land, owned the XL, the biggest ranch in the county, and the town's only saloon and whorehouse. Soon, he hoped to get his hands on Gila Crossing's general store. Then it would be his town. He laid on big parties, drink and female companionship free, for the notable citizens of the town and it was not long before Mr Jackson Pearson's name was being bandied about by the leading citizens as warranting high office at the county seat.

Petch smiled. For some unexpected reason he was thinking of two years back, of how surprised Raynor, Santos and the other two boys must have looked just before they were gunned down knowing they wouldn't be getting any of the gold. His smile widened. But what the hell, he thought, the bastards would have only wasted their cut on rotgut whiskey, two-dollar whores and crooked poker games. They wouldn't have striven for the finer things in life, rich living and power.

A husky voice calling out, 'Are you comin' back into bed, honey, I'm gettin' cold lyin' here,' brought Petch back to thinking even pleasanter thoughts. Though he did wonder how Ringold and his boys were faring below the border, stealing horses and cattle from Mexican *rancheros* to build up his herd a lot cheaper than buying the longhorns legally at cattle sales. Mr 'Pearson' hadn't altogether given up earning a fast buck the owlhoot way. He walked back into the bedroom, shrugging off his dressing-gown as he reached the big, four-poster bed and the invitingly smiling Elizabeta stretched out on it as bare-fleshed as he was.

3

Raynor and Santos were intending to cross over into Arizona at a quieter spot than the regular crossing at Nogales where they would be fingered by the border guards as *pistoleros*. While there were no outstanding warrants for the pair in Arizona, some eagle-eyed lawman might recognize them as members of the Petch gang — a risk they were not willing to take.

They rode in silence, deep in their own thoughts, thinking of their coming violent encounter with Petch, the wiping out of a long, bitterly held score. Raynor was having second thoughts about riding into Gila Crossing and, at the first sighting of Petch, hauling out their pistols and sending him winging on his way to Hell, and then ass-kicking it back into Sonora and safety.

'*Compadre*,' he said, 'I know we've

both got a good reason to kill Petch pronto like, but that action won't get us any of our dinero back. We'll have raised a hornets' nest and still be broke. And we're getting too old in the tooth to take up robbin' banks again. If that fella's right about Petch ownin' a saloon and a whorehouse, why, they'll have safes.' He grinned. 'Office safes are easier to open than bank vaults, *amigo*. Then we'll burn down Petch's money-makin' businesses.'

Santos, feeling the strain of the long ride only gave him a bleary-eyed look.

'It don't mean that we ain't goin' to shoot the sonuvabitch,' Raynor added quickly, sensing that his partner didn't altogether agree with his tactics. 'We'll be hittin' him were it hurts, in his pocket. Get him confused about who the hell's poking a sharp stick in his eye. Then we'll pick our time to take what he's got locked up in his ranch house, before we shoot him dead. OK, *compadre*?'

Before Santos could give his opinion

on his partner's suggestion, they heard the distant rattle of gunfire, a sound that cleared the trail weariness from them.

'Trouble for someone, *amigo*,' Raynor said. 'And no business of ours. Our trouble lies across there in Arizona.' He took his partner's grunt as agreement of his view.

Ten minutes' ride closer to the border, they had to pull up their horses to a walk to allow them to pick their way through scores of sheep milling about on the trail. Once clear of the herd, they saw what the firing had been all about. Three Mexicans, one of them a mere boy, lay in crumpled heaps by a campfire.

Santos gave a muttered curse and rode ahead of the dead sheepherders camp. Raynor drew out his Spencer and kept a keen-eyed watch all around him. He saw Santos lean over to examine the ground more closely before riding back to join him.

His face as savage as any Yaqui's he

said, 'I will bury these *pacificos*, Juan, then I will ride and catch up with the cattle stealers, gringos by the reading of the horse tracks, who shot them down like dogs.' He gave Raynor a stone-eyed look. 'This is Mexican business, *compadre*, my business. You ride on to Arizona and kill Petch, or wait there until I join you then we will carry out your plan of taking from Petch what belongs to us.'

'You saw cattle tracks then, heading' north?' Raynor said.

Santos nodded. 'A sizeable herd, *amigo*, so the gringo pigs will not be moving fast.'

Raynor could see the grim pattern of events that had led to the slaying of the three Mexicans. The sheepherders had unfortunately made their camp on the trail the stolen herd was being driven along and had been shot down like dogs, as Santos had said, so they could not describe the likenesses of the Yankee rustlers to the *rurale* border patrols. The way the rustlers would see it was that it was no big deal killing three greasers if it meant saving them from a hanging. *Bandido* or not, Santos was proud of his race and Raynor could understand his natural need to avenge his countrymen's deaths, killings that called for blood for blood. Just as natural, with him being Santos's partner, he would ride with him.

'We'll dig the graves, *amigo*,' he said, hard-voiced. 'Then we will catch up with the gringos who did this terrible deed. Petch will still be in Gila Crossing when we do what we're beholden to do.' He thrust the Spencer back into its boot and dismounted.

★ ★ ★

Rinegold was feeling in high spirits. He was driving at least 250 head of prime cattle lifted from a Don's *ranchero* and the Arizona border could be no more that ten miles or so ahead of them. Frank North, riding point, hadn't come racing back so there must be no *rurale* patrol between them and Arizona. There had been a slight hitch back along the trail a piece when they had passed close by a greaser sheepherders' camp. Ringegold grinned. As the saying goes, he thought, dead men can't point the finger.

Santos and Raynor put their mounts under the lash once they had roughly covered the bodies of the sheepherders with stones. The sheep would come to no harm; there was plenty of grass and water close by for their needs until the peons from where the sheepherders, lived came out to check on their *compañeros*. They had to get ahead of the herd before it was driven across the border. Their plan, made quickly as they thundered across the plain, was to try and turn the herd, sparking them into a stampede and, in the noisy, dusty chaos that would raise, gun down as many of the rustlers as they could without endangering their own revenge-seeking plans.

'There the sonsuvbitches are!'

Raynor called out, nodding towards the dust haze ahead of them.

They both swung their mounts down into a shallow, sun-baked arroya bottom, reckoning that the drag men bringing up the rear of the herd would be regularly casting glances along their back trail looking for the dust of any pursuing riders.

Frank North was the first rustler to feel the hand of vengeance tap him on the shoulder. He was still riding point well ahead of the herd, sitting easy in his saddle as he thought of how he was going to spend his cut of the price Rinegold would get for the herd from rancher Pearson. He abruptly stopped his ruminating and straightened up in his saddle, hand resting on the butt of his pistol, as he saw two riders coming towards him.

As they closed in on him he noticed that one of them was a thickset, ugly-faced Mexican whose sombrero brim looked as though rats, or other suchlike vermin, had chewed lumps out of it. His partner was a tall stern-faced Yankee and he didn't look like he was dressed to go to some dance. North calculated that the pair were saddle tramps, spineless drifters too idle to seek sweat-raising work. There was no need to fire off warning shots to alert Ringold and the boys that he had hit trouble.

'*Buenos dias, señor*,' Santos said, a smile cracking his leathery face as he pulled alongside the point man. Raynor held slightly back. This was his partner's play; he didn't want to jeopardize his actions by crowding in on the rustler on his other side and alarm him any.

'Me and my gringo *compadre*,' continued Santos, still showing his painfully forced grin, 'wondered if you have any spare *tabac*? We're kind of short of the dinero . . . ' he finished lamely.

North grinned to himself. He had guessed right, the pair were stony broke saddle tramps.

'I've got some of your greaser cigarillos in my saddle-bag,' he said. He reached round behind him to loosen the straps on the bag, turning slightly away from Santos as he did so. It was the break Santos had been hoping for. He struck with the deadly speed of a disturbed rattler. His right hand came up from beneath his *serape* and the machete it gripped flashed coldly in the sunlight. The vicious back-handed sweep almost decapitated North in a fearful spout of blood. His horse, smelling the blood, snorted with splayed-nostril fear and began stiff-legged bucking that threw its lifeless rider out of his saddle to land with a dull thud like a burst feed sack on to the ground.

Raynor cold-smiled. 'That was slick work,' he said. 'Now let's get started on turnin' those cows comin' up, *amigo*.' He sniffed at the air. 'The wind's in our favour.'

Rinegold, riding as one of the right swing men, came over the slight rise in the trail to see the line of smoking flames being wind-driven towards the herd.

'Christ Almighty!' he yelled. 'A prairie fire!' and pulled up his horse in a neck-jerking halt. Before he could think of how the herd could outflank the wall of fire the leading longhorns came up with their own solution to get themselves out of danger. Bellowing, they turned round in a whirl of kicked-up dust. Stamping and jostling, they tried to break through the cows behind them. Then the rest of the herd caught the smell of the smoke and spooked, out of control of Ringold and his eight-man crew.

A cursing Ringold knew he had lost the herd; the cows would be spread halfway across Sonora before they stopped raising the dust, dust that could be seen by *rurale* patrols. When the last of the herd thundered past him, he yelled out, 'The cows are lost, boys! Let's get clear of that fire and head for home before some Mex lawmen show up!'

The two men bringing up the drag were not fast enough to get clear of the stampeding longhorns, they and their horses went down in a welter of blood and crunched bones. It was a bad time for Ringold. He had lost his spending money the runaway cattle would have brought him, and two of his boys were dead. Maybe three, he thought gloomily, North hadn't ridden back in. Now all they could do was to save their own necks by cutting around the edge of the line of fire, hoping to hell that the blaze hadn't aroused the Mexican border patrols, or he and his boys would have a real killing fight on their hands to make it back to Arizona.

The gang turned north again where the flames had petered out on a rocky outcrop and spurred their frightened horses across the fire-blackened ground. Then Ringold discovered just how bad a time it was for him and his boys. Gunfire sounded to the right of them and three of his men were shot off their mounts. Through the drifting smoke he saw gun flashes and quickly realized that the fire hadn't been caused by the hand of God. He had no idea who had ambushcd them, but whoever they were they had the edge. His crew was in no position to make a stand and fight back. It was cut-and-run-for-it time. Crouching low, Indian style, they raced to get clear of the deadly rifle fire.

The two smoke-blackened-faced *compadres* grinned at each other. They had counted three men brought down by their rifles and between them and the far line of the dying out fires they could see two smouldering bundles, which could only be two more of the cattle-lifting gang.

'As we figured,' Santos said. 'The sonsuvbitches rode right across the front of our guns.'

'Yeah. They took what they thought was the shortest way around the fire,' replied Raynor. He nodded towards the three gunshot rustlers. 'It was the shortest way to Hell for those fellas. Those sheepherders will rest easy in their graves, I reckon. Now let's be on our way; we ain't raisin' a sweat buryin' gringo killers and there could be *rurales* comin' this way at any time.'

Ringold, and what was left of his gang, kept up their neck-risking gallop until they had put the border well behind them. On their slower pace to Gila Crossing, Ringold began to ponder on just who it was who had all but wiped out his gang. How could he, he thought angrily, do any serious cattle lifting with just two men.

He had picked at least two rifles cutting loose at them through the smoke. If there had only been two men then it couldn't have been *rurales* who had ambushed them. Those bastards rode in small armies and wouldn't have needed to light any fires; they would have ridden in on them guns blazing. They could have been Yankee lawmen. He had heard that sometimes Texas Rangers operated south of the Rio Grande, but Arizona wasn't Texas. Were they part of a rival cattle-lifting gang who wanted to take over his good-paying business? Ringold was still trying to work out who the riflemen could have been when they reached the outskirts of Gila Crossing.

4

Jonas Curry, standing on his porch, was still in shock. He didn't know whether to curse or burst into tears at his sudden, bad turn of fortune. Mr P.T. Sutton, Gila Crossing's one, and only lawyer, had left not ten minutes ago after telling him that he could lose his farm, land he and Martha, his wife, and the kids, when they came of age, had sweated blood to cultivate. Earning enough, in a good growing year, to put a bit by.

'Your original loan was from old Colonel Sanderson, Mr Curry, on very favourable terms, I may add,' the mealy-mouthed bastard had said. 'Now the colonel has passed away I have instructions from his next of kin, a nephew who resides in St Louis, who inherited his estate, to sell the big house, its contents and any other land or property his uncle owned as soon as

42

a buyer can be found. Mister Jackson Pearson has come forward with the asking price, a very substantial sum indeed. Naturally Mr Pearson wants to regain some of the capital he's laid out by selling parts of the estate he can no longer run at a loss. Such as your farm, Mr Curry. On checking the records I have noticed that you are well behind in your mortgage payments.'

'But the colonel let — ' Jonas began.

'Yes, yes, I know that the colonel allowed you to defer payment until you sold your crops,' interrupted P.T. Sutton, 'but legally you have broken your agreement by not meeting your commitment on the dates stated in the contract, so by law this land reverts to its new owner, Mr Pearson.'

Jonas's head was swimming trying to take in all the forked-tongued legal jargon the shyster was spouting. Why didn't he just come out with the plain truth? Mr Jackson Pearson, the big man in the county wanted to grab another section of land.

P.T. Sutton favoured Jonas with a lawyer's oily, skindeep smile. 'Now Mr Pearson is not a hard man,' he said, 'and doesn't wish to appear unreasonable by seeming to be forcing a man off his land he's worked for years so he's allowing you three months' grace in which time he expects you to have cleared off the outstanding payments owing to him. Then he will no doubt ask me to draw up a new contract with you enabling you to hold on to your property. Failing to meet that deadline will mean I will have to issue an eviction order.' P.T. Sutton's sympathetic look had the shallowness of his smile.

A numb-nerved Jonas watched the lawyer's buggy pull away, then it was cursing or crying time.

How the hell could he come up with the back payments in three months, he thought frantically? Rob a goddamned bank? He and his family eat grass for the next year? Though, he admitted grudgingly, what P.T. Sutton had told

44

him was all legal and above board. He had held on to his land for so long by the generosity of the old colonel, for having saved his life at the battle of Shiloh when he had fallen badly wounded storming the Rebs' second line of defences. Jackson Pearson owed him no suchlike favours. Though that didn't make it any easier for him to tell Martha and the kids that they were about to lose all they had in the world.

★　★　★

'Now we've got to come up with some sort of a plan, *amigo*,' Raynor said. 'We must be getting close to this Gila Crossing and we don't want to be riding along Main Street just as Petch is stepping out of some bar or bang goes our hopes of gettin' our money from the bastard because we'll have no choice but to gun him down. Then, as I said, we'll have to hightail it south havin' only done half what we've ridden this far to do.'

'But we will have to risk showin' our faces in Gila Crossing, *amigo*,' replied Santos. 'We have to eat.' He thin-smiled. 'And m'be pay for the services of a gringo *señorita*.'

'Yeah, I can *comprende* the eatin' part,' Raynor said. 'But gettin' this close to that sonuvabitch kinda dampens any urge I've got for female company.'

They came to a field of ripening corn and, skirting around one edge, met up with a deep rutted track that led to a shack and several outbuildings. They nosed their mounts along the trail.

A glum-faced Jonas came out of the barn knowing that he could not put off any longer telling his family the bad news that soon they would be homeless. All his anger was directed at Jackson Pearson. God Almighty, he thought, the taking bastard as well as owning the old colonel's land had the biggest cattle spread in the territory, a saloon, and a cat house. And the talk in the town had it that his grabbing hands were reaching out for Saul Farrow's general store.

What the hell was the urgency for him to want his place, he thought angrily? He couldn't sell it as a going farm. All the dirt farmers hereabouts were in debt to the bank; they couldn't afford to buy another holding.

Jonas saw two riders watering their horses at the creek. Men who were strangers to him. That's all he needed to make his day, he thought bitterly, two asshole drifters calling on him for a handout. As the riders came up the grade to the house, Jonas got a closer look at his univited visitors. The leading rider sat tall in the saddle, an American, his partner was a broad-shouldered Mexican with a face, Jonas opined, no amount of smiling would soften. He had seen sweeter-looking Apache broncos. He hurried on to the house to face them standing on the porch alongside the loaded shotgun that stood there.

They drew up their mounts well short of the cabin and remained in their saddles. Raynor could see by the homesteader's scowling look that he wasn't overjoyed at seeing them.

'I hope we ain't stoppin' you from your chores, mister,' Raynor said smiling. 'But we'd be rightly obliged if you could point me and my pard in the direction of Mr Jackson Pearson's spread. We've heard he's hirin' men,' Raynor thought it would be wiser to ask about Petch's whereabouts from someone out in the backwoods than asking openly in Gila Crossing.

'Yeah, I reckon the bastard will be needing a bigger crew the way he's buildin' up his herd,' Jonas replied. 'If you follow the trail northwards you'll come out on the XL ranch's home range; you'll be able to see the big house. Or you could catch up with Pearson in town. He spends a lot of time watching the dollars roll into the tills in the Long Branch, the saloon he owns, when he's not pleasurin' the madam of the local cat house, which belongs to him as well.'

'Mr Pearson seems to be a big man in Gila Crossing,' Raynor said. By his scowl it seemed that the sodbuster wasn't favourably minded towards the former Jake Petch.

'You'd better believe it, mister,' Jonas replied. 'He owns the only saloon, the cat house, the local law and the town's lawyer. The only business he don't own on Main Street is the bank and Saul Farrow's general store. And I reckon that Pearson will get his grabbin' hands on that soon. The last wagonload of Farrow's supplies, hauled by wagon from the rail depot was ambushed, and the driver told Farrow that he was paid to drive the wagon not to be accosted by road agents who threatened to shoot him if they saw him haulin' freight again. Now I ain't sayin' that Pearson had anything to do with Farrow losin' his supplies, but he never had any trouble gettin' in his new goods before Pearson showed up in the territory.'

Then Jonas's suppressed anger at losing his farm broke through, in front of strangers, and as stone-faced as any men he had ever clapped eyes on.

'Pearson, the sonuvabitch, is takin' this place from me, this house I built and all the land I've worked!' The words came rushing out. 'Just because I owe him a few months' back rent!'

'Is that true, Pa?' cried a white-faced Martha who had stepped out of the cabin on hearing her husband talking to someone. 'Mr Pearson is taking our home?'

'That's what lawyer Sutton told me, Ma,' Jonas replied.

Martha ran back into the cabin, sobbing loudly. Jonas, grim-faced, followed her in.

'Petch is still the asshole he always was, José,' Raynor said. 'If he spends a great deal of his time in town it'll be wise of us to sneak in there just to check things out.' He grinned. 'I'll make the trip. The way you're armed up, *amigo*, strollin' along Main Street you'll have the sheriff and his deputies out on the street thinking that a bloodthirsty Mexican *bandido jefe* has hit his town. If Petch is in town and sees what's goin' on then we've lost the edge over the sonuvabitch. Knowin' how Petch thinks, he'll take it that you're not on your own trackin' him down. He'll have more men guardin' him than the President.'

Another reason Raynor didn't want Santos riding into town was that his *compadre* could backslide and start downing the tequila again. And a mad-ass drunk Santos would raise hell in Gila Crossing, shooting at anyone who took his fancy.

'OK,' Santos growled. 'We'll play it your way, *amigo*.'

They pulled their horses round from the house and rode southwards along the creek, trusting that it would lead to Gila Crossing. Raynor didn't want to annoy the farmer by asking him the directions to the town, not when the poor bastard would be trying to comfort his family.

5

Raynor rode into Gila Crossing on his own, no longer looking like a gringo. He was wearing Santos's *serape* and drooping-brimmed sombrero, pulled low down on his face, and his belt of reloads slung across his chest, a disguise that would not only fool the townsfolk but Petch himself, unless he came up to him real close.

On the outskirts of the town, they had run into a Mexican sheepherders' camp of at least eight families' strength. An ideal spot for Santos to lie low while Raynor, as they had decided, took a look around Gila Crossing.

Raynor drew up his mount outside the Long Branch saloon, Jackson Pearson's place, betting on the fact that if Pearson stepped out he wouldn't give the tall greaser a second glance. Opposite was the general store whose owner, according to the sodbuster they had called on, was having a bellyful of trouble. He saw several men lifting a man's body out of the bed of a wagon and a small worried-faced man wearing a store-clerk's apron directing them to take the man into the store. Raynor heard him call out, 'Get the doc, pronto, and the sheriff!' The storekeeper's trouble was still with him.

Curious, he dismounted, but not wanting to draw attention to himself — greasers didn't poke their noses into a gringo's affair — he just stood and watched. It was not long before one of the men who had been helping to carry the body came across the street eager to tell the gawpers standing on the saloon porch about Farrow's latest upset. How he had lost another full wagonload of supplies and that old Pete had been badly shot up.

'The sheriff reckons the ambush and the shootin' of Pete could be the work of greaser bad-asses raidin' from across the border,' the news spreader said, and he cast a suspicious look at Raynor. 'Whoever it is, it's ruinin' Farrow's business. That's the second load of supplies he's had stolen. He'll never be able to hire another driver for his wagon to make the trip to the rail depot and risk gettin' shot on the trail back.'

If the taking of Farrow's stores was the work of road agents, Mexican or gringo, Raynor thought, then he'd take up religion. As the sodbuster had hinted, Petch was behind the storekeeper's trouble. Petch intended going places and he would shoot anyone who stood in his way. The son-of-a-bitch had gunned down his own gang to get here. The storekeeper would be wise to sit up all night with a loaded shotgun across his knees to make sure his store didn't 'accidentally' go up in flames. He slow-smiled. A hard-up greaser might be desperate enough to pick up the wagon's reins. It could be the start of the trouble he and Santos was going to heap on Petch.

A big-bellied, cigar-smoking man in

shirt sleeves, sporting a fancy vest, came out of the saloon and watched the scene at the store. It took all of Raynor's self-control for him not to yank out his pistol and shoot down Petch where he stood. He had no doubt that if Santos had been with him, he wouldn't have hesitated one little bit in shooting Petch. Then the pair of them would be rib-kicking it back across into old Mexico ahead of a hanging posse, and no damn richer. He saw Petch's greedy-eyed look, and if Raynor had any thoughts that some road agents passing through the territory had stolen the stores and shot the driver, he knew he would have been thinking wrong. The storekeeper was about to get himself a new driver. Keeping his back to Petch he walked across to the store.

Saul Farrow's face set in hard, determined lines. His grandpappy had started the business when Gila Crossing had only been a backwoods settlement. Then his pa had taken over the store and, on his death, some ten years ago,

Farrow's General Store had been his. He'd be damned if he would let some rich stranger to the territory buy him out. Though looking at things as they were, if the next wagon of supplies, due at the depot at the end of the week, was stolen he would go bust. That was, of course, assuming that he could hire a driver.

The sheriff had been no help telling him that if he had the deputies to spare to ride shotgun with the wagon it would be a waste of time because the sons-of-bitches wouldn't attack it. They would wait until the escort had been withdrawn before they started stealing his supplies again.

'You could buy yourself a coupla hired guns, Saul,' the sheriff had said. 'But you'd be wastin' your money; the same thing would happen; the *bandidos* would lie low till the coast was clear then swoop in on the wagon again. M'be you oughta take up Mr Pearson's offer for the store.'

Saul Farrow gave a muttered, 'Like

hell I will,' to the sheriff's back as he walked out. He would make a pact with the Devil if it would prevent Pearson grabbing hold of the store. On the other hand the *bandidos* could have moved to do their robbing someplace else. He would find out the next trip for supplies because he would be up on the wagon himself.

He looked at the sound of a grating voice saying, 'I will drive your wagon, Señor Farrow.' Words he had never expected to hear again.

Standing just inside the store was a tall, armed to the teeth, mean-faced Mexican, and he got a peculiar feeling that he was gazing at a devil, maybe not Old Nick himself, but evil-looking enough to raise several kinds of hell. That is if he didn't head south with the goods to give his wife and kids free meals. Though what could he lose, Farrow thought? Either the road agents would take his supplies, or the big greaser would and his shelves would soon be bare and he would cease to trade. Or he could drive the wagon himself and get what old Pete got, or worse, and Pearson would get the store for chicken feed. He had to admit that the Mexican had the cut of a *pistolero* and was more likely to beat off any attack on the wagon than he could.

He managed a weak grin. 'You're hired, *señor*, er . . . '

'*Muchas gracias*,' Raynor replied. Baring his teeth in a wolf-like snarl of a grin he added, 'You will not lose your supplies, Señor Farrow. I, Pablo Castro, promise you that!'

Farrow again eyed the big cannon of a pistol sheathed on his new driver's right hip, and the wicked-looking machete swinging at his other side, the rifle held high across his chest and believed what he had told him, his supplies would be safe with him.

'There will be a load of supplies to be picked up at the depot in three days' time, Señor Castro,' he said. The mules will be hitched up and ready to roll out at nine o'clock.' With the Mexican's fearsome presence still unsettling him, Farrow thought it wise to show his new hiring a little respect. 'And I'll pay you your due right now,' he said.

'*Nada*, pay me when I return with your supplies, *señor*,' replied Raynor. And the storekeeper got another glimpse of the 'Mexican's' death's-head grin. 'And the body of any *bandido* who tries to take them.' Raynor touched the brim of his sombrero in a farewell gesture and, with a jangling of spurs, strode out into the street leaving a morose-looking Farrow thinking that he was gambling his future on the gun expertise of an unknown ragged-assed Mexican drifter.

6

An impassive-faced Petch sat back in the big chair in his private room at the rear of the Long Branch saloon listening to Ringold telling him how the last cattle raid had gone all to hell with the shooting down of six of his men.

'I don't know who the sonuvabitches were who jumped us,' Ringold said to the man he knew as Mr Pearson. 'Or how many of them, but I do know for sure they weren't after the herd; they scattered the cows all across Sonora. They were after killin' me and my boys. Thinkin' of who could be wantin' to spill my blood has kinda got me puzzled, Mr Pearson.'

Ringold had been eager to tell Pearson of the attack and his worries as soon as he had come into town but Pearson was on his ranch and Ringold, being a man wanted by the law in several counties in the state, had strict orders from Pearson, who had high political hopes, not to meet up with him in public. Seen consorting with outlaws wouldn't help him on the road to the state capital any. Here, in the saloon, it was easy for Ringold to slip away from the bar unnoticed into Pearson's office.

Petch was as puzzled as Ringold was about whom the ambushers could have been and was naturally disappointed that the herd had been lost. They could have been a bunch of border bad-asses settling some old grievance with Ringold. It made no difference to his plans; there were still plenty of cows for the taking in Sonora. And the men who would do the lifting came a dime a dozen hereabouts. Ringold would soon have a gang again.

'Hire as many men as you need to take up cattle-raidin' again, Ringold,' he said. 'But hold back for a spell before ridin' south. In the meantime, scout around and ask questions,' Petch smiled, 'of fellas in your line of business to see if they've been ambushed on a raid. The men who put your boys down smell like cattlemen's regulators, but I've never heard of Yankee regulators operatin' in Mexico. I'll ask the sheriff to see if he's heard official that regulators are at work in his bailiwick.'

'I'll do that, Mr Pearson,' Ringegold said, hard-voiced. 'I've some reckonin' to do with those bastards, regulators or whoever. Six dead boys' worth.'

Petch allowed time for Ringegold to get bellied up to the bar once more, reckoning that things on the whole were going pretty smoothly for him. He judged that the shooting of Farrow's wagon driver would have the store-keeper willing to accept his terms for taking the store off his hands. Then he would get the shyster, P.T. Sutton, to go through all the county land registry records to see if there was any loophole by which he could claim the land of the few cattle ranchers close to Gila Crossing. Maybe have Ringegold and his new gang put pressure on the ranchers, like stealing their cattle or burning their barns, to make them quit the cattle-raising trade. Petch smiled to himself. A man who ran cattle over half the county ought to have a clear run to making state governor.

On seeing his boss coming into the bar, the head barkeep placed a bottle of his favourite whiskey and a glass at his usual end of the bar. Grinning all over his face he said, 'You won't have heard yet, Mr Pearson, but Saul Farrow has just hired himself a greaser as his wagon driver.'

Petch paused in his pouring out a shot of whiskey. Farrow was still stubbornly hanging on to his store. But only until he found out that he had lost another load of supplies and a driver shot dead. That is if the Mexican didn't leap off the wagon and hightail it back across the border when Stilson and his two cousins, men on his payroll, bushwhacked him. Though the three blood kin men couldn't be classed as top ranch hands, they were good at clearing any hitches on his ride to being the main man in the territory, the hard, painful way for whoever was slowing his progress.

He turned from the bar and, raising his voice, called out above the noise of the saloon. 'Boys, I've just heard that Mr Farrow has hired himself a Mex driver to face those road agents who are hijackin' his supplies. Now if that bold-hearted greaser hauls in the wagon with Mr Farrow's goods still stacked on it he can drink his fill at this bar, on the house!'

'It would be kinder, Mr Pearson, runnin' a fund for the poor bastard's widow!' a drinker at the bar shouted.

Ain't that the truth, a smiling Petch thought as he poured himself out a generous measure of whiskey.

7

Although Raynor left early to pick up the stores there were at least a dozen or so men standing outside the saloon watching him pull out. All of them liked a gamble, but none of them was prepared to risk a red cent on a hundred to one wager that the Mexican would come back with Farrow's stores. But all gave the greaser an ironic cheer and calls of, 'Good luck, Mex!' as the wagon rolled out.

Raynor, still playing the role of an easy-going Mexican, slouched back on the seat and let the two mules pick up their own pace; his own horse was tied to the tailgate. He didn't expect trouble until the return journey with the wagon loaded, but as relaxed as he looked he was ready to meet it any time it came. A pistol was laid across his knees, his second pistol, covered by a piece of tarp, lay on the seat alongside him. Leaning against his leg, butt resting on the floor, was his Spencer, with a shell already levered into the firing chamber.

Somewhere ahead of him and to the right of the trail, though he hadn't even raised as much as a wisp of dust, was Santos. Also all gunned up. Both of them being longtime experts in the art of bushwhacking, he was confident that no road agents could surprise him.

He had told Farrow that he wouldn't be able to stay in Gila Crossing as he had to attend to a wife seriously ill in a village just across the Mexican border. But he would return the morning he was due to pick up the supplies. As he rode out of Gila Crossing, Raynor smiled. By the look the storekeeper had given him as he left the store he had been thinking that he would never see his newly hired wagon driver again, that Raynor would've had second thoughts about risking his life to help out a Yankee storekeeper.

Raynor had made for the sheepherders' camp to tell Santos that they were about to start their war against Petch. Though he didn't tell his partner that he had been close enough to Petch to have slipped a knife between his ribs. He didn't want him to be harbouring unsettling thoughts so as to dull his reactions when the time came to throw down on the wagon raiders and kill them. Instead, he explained to Santos how the storekeeper had lost his last load of goods and had his driver badly shot up.

'That sodbuster was right, José,' he said. 'It ain't road agents who are takin' that storekeeper's goods, it's men hired by our own boss.' He grinned. 'I've got myself hired as a wagon driver; I'm pickin' up the next load of supplies from the rail depot. Between us we oughta be able to spring a nasty surprise on those *bandidos* if they try to jump me. It could upset Petch's grand plan somewhat, m'be enough to cause him a few sleepless nights.'

Raynor's grin this time held no warmth at all. 'While Petch is tryin' to figure out the new situation he's got facin' him,' he continued, 'we'll take the cash from the safes in the saloon and the whorehouse, then torch the buildin's. Then, *mi amigo*, we will ride out to Petch's ranch house, kill him and take what cash he's holdin' there. But it won't be for four days before I take the wagon out and I can't stay all that time in Gila Crossin' or they'll find out I ain't a Mexican. I told the storekeeper I'm livin' in a village just across the border, looking after my sick wife. I would be obliged if you could ask your countrymen if they wouldn't be too put out allowin' a gringo to share their camp.'

'There is a corner of the hut where I sleep where a gringo could lay out his bedroll if he don't mind eating tortillas for every meal,' replied Santos.

Raynor grinned. 'I don't mind, *amigo*. It's a long, long time since someone cooked chow, of any kind, for me.'

★ ★ ★

It was time for the rail depot superintendent's siesta when Raynor drove the wagon into the depot's stockade. Normally he would have forgone fifteen minutes or so of his high-noon shuteye to hear the latest news and gossip from Farrow's wagon driver about the goings on back there in Gila Crossing, but with the storekeeper sending word yesterday that his driver was a Mexican he didn't think it worth delaying pulling off his boots and lying down on his cot. He gave instructions for his clerk to see to the paperwork regarding Farrow's stores, but did stay long enough at his office window before he took his nap to have a look at the greaser who was about to commit suicide. Then again, he thought, most greasers were crazy with living under this goddamned sun all their lives.

Raynor locked the tailgate and climbed on to the wagon seat and picked up the reins. As he was about to kick off the brake he heard the elderly Mexican, who had been helping him load the wagon say, '*Amigo*, you are one loco *hombre* to risk your life for a gringo. There are *bandidos* along the Gila Crossing trail.'

Raynor pushed back his sombrero and winked at the old man.

'*Madre de Dios*!' the old man gasped, stepping back from the wagon as it jerked forward. The big Mexican wasn't a Mexican but a gringo! Why he was posing as one had him puzzled. Though he had to admit the actions of most Yankees were a mystery to him.

★　★　★

'Here it comes, boys,' Stilson said, as he caught sight of the wagon's trail dust. 'It ain't fair for us to shoot down that greaser from behind these rocks.' He grinned. 'We'll go right on to the trail and scare the crap outa him before we gun him down.'

Raynor saw the three riders come

from out of the rockfall to block the progress of the wagon. None of them had his pistol fisted or held his long gun on him. He gave a twist of a grin. His disguise must be working. They would be thinking that a Mexican facing three gringo bad-asses would have him leaping off the wagon and running for cover. Then the bastards would hunt him down and shoot him dead just for the fun of it.

He drew up the wagon within pistol range of the three grinning road agents then reached for his guns. 'José!' he yelled out. 'Leave the sonuvabitch on the grey to me!'

Stilson, the son-of-a-bitch on the grey, had only time for a flash of a 'What the hell', surprised look at his two partners, when Santos's first shot took off half of Billy Jack's face in a fearful welter of blood and bone, flinging him out of his saddle. Two loads from Raynor's pistol drove into Stilson's chest folding him over his saddlehorn drowning in his own blood, too far gone to register the second shot from the men who had outfoxed them that tore a killing hole through his other blood kin's back.

A grinning Santos picked his way down through the rocks, rifle held in one hand. '*Pistoleros*,' he growled, and spat at one of the bodies. 'It was an easy kill, *amigo*,' he said, as he came up to the wagon.

Raynor smiled. 'Don't be too hard on the sonsuvbitches, José. They thought they were only facin' a chicken-livered *pacifico* and m'be reckoned they could make me eat crow before pluggin' me. Now go and get your horse, I'll finish things up here before any rider comes along the trail. Those fellas back there in Gila Crossing will be wonderin' how the loco greaser is makin' out and one of them might be curious enough to ride out for a looksee.'

As Raynor drove the now wagon-cum-hearse back towards Gila Crossing, Santos riding alongside, Raynor said, 'What we've done here, *compadre*, must start Petch worryin' about who the hell the tall Mexican is and how he could get the better of three armed men, and what's his game? Then the bastard will be bound to set up a big hunt for this fast-shootin' Mexican and the first place they'll look for him is the sheepherders' camp so I'll have to make myself scarce.'

'You don't figure on cold camping it until we're ready to take on Petch, *amigo?*' Santos said.

No,' replied Raynor. 'I'm bankin' on more men than Farrow who don't like Petch's way of doin' business who'd be willin' to put me up for a spell. Petch won't think that the tall greaser would be crazy enough to stay close to town. We'll pay a call on that storekeeper and sound him out about findin' me a place to hole-up.' He grinned. 'And collect the due he owes me for bringin' in his stores. Meanwhile, we'll drive the wagon to within sight of the town and then let the mules take it in on their own.

8

A cry of, 'Your wagon's comin' in, Mr
Farrow!' from one of the growing
crowd outside the store had Farrow
rushing out on to his porch, eyeballing
anxiously the moving cloud of dust
being raised on the west trail. For the
last hour or so when he opined that the
Mexican should be on his way back, if
everything had gone OK, he had
resisted the urge to go out on to the
street and look for signs of the wagon's
approach. Instead, he had shifted goods
here and there, anything to keep
himself from thinking that in a short
while he would know whether or not he
was still in business. The odds, he had
painfully to admit, were on the grasping
hands of Jackson Pearson taking over
his store. He couldn't tell from this
distance if the wagon was loaded and
the Mexican was still up on the driving

seat, or if there had been another raid and a fresh grave had to be dug on Boot Hill.

There was such excitement among the waiting men over the outcome of the Mexican's trip to the depot that small sums of cash were being wagered on whether the greaser would be bringing in Farrow's supplies, or if he had paid for his bravado and ended up like old Pete. Petch had opened up his saloon early to ease the gamblers' thirsts and was now standing on the boardwalk contemplating the changes to the store the Stilson cousins had handed to him on a plate.

A keener-eyed watcher yelled, 'The wagon's loaded, and I can see three horses in tow.' Then, puzzled voiced, he added, 'But I'm damned if I can see the Mex up on the wagon!'

Right now Farrow didn't give a hoot if the Mexican was driving the wagon or dead somewhere along the trail, his supplies were coming in, that was all that concerned him. Later on, when he got over the good feeling that he still had a business, he would feel more charitable towards the fate of the big Mexican. If he was dead he could maybe find out what village his sick wife lived in and send her her husband's due. But right now it was, kiss-my-ass smiling time across at Jackson Pearson standing there outside his saloon.

The mules, well used to the trip to the depot and back, stopped outside the store and all the waiting men got their first glimpse of the grisly load the wagon was carrying. Stretched across the crates of stores were the bodies of three well and truly gunshot dead men. Stilson, Jack and Bewick, men they had bellied up to the saloon bar with. Men who worked as ranch hands for Mr Jackson Pearson, and who must have been the road agents who had been taking Farrow's stores. There was a stunned, hard to believe silence, then everyone spoke at once. Had the big greaser killed them on his own? Where was he now? Why had he not brought the wagon in?

Petch was also wondering where the Mexican was, and, more worrying to him, who he was. He must be part of a gang of *bandidos*, he thought; one man couldn't have got the best of Stilson and his two men. But if he was a Mexican bad-ass why had he not taken Farrow's stores? One thing was for sure, he'd have to do some heavy lying because the whole town knew that the three dead men on the wagon were on his payroll.

As he turned to walk back into the saloon, Petch suddenly began to link this trouble with the killing trouble Ringold had had in Sonora. Did Farrow's Mexican have a hand in that business? If so then he had big trouble on his hands, trouble that was beginning to chew painfully away at his guts because the bastards who were targeting him knew him as Petch. Ringold could have been unlucky to have had a run in with a *rurale* patrol or some home-raised cattle lifters in Sonora, but

Farrow hadn't the money to hire a top *pistolero*, gringo or Mexican, so the tall Mexican had taken on driving the wagon to scotch his plans for taking over the store. That had Petch puzzled, and worried. The only Mexican he had done the dirty on was the ugly-faced Santos and he'd been lying dead in some godforsaken creek a couple of years now. Or was he? The pain in his guts spread. He inclined his head slightly at Ringegold standing at the far end of the bar then walked on into his private office.

'Come along, boys,' Farrow said. 'Give me a hand to get these thievin' bastards' bodies on to the board-walk; they're the sheriff's business now. Then help me to unload the stores. I'll buy drinks for you all when we've finished.' He glared across at the saloon. 'Once he's seen to the bodies, the sheriff can go across to the saloon and ask Mr Jackson Pearson how it comes that three men on his payroll have been stealin' my stores and almost killed old Pete.'

In his office, a grim-faced Petch was giving Ringold fresh and urgent orders. 'Lay off the liftin' of Mexican cattle,' he said. 'I want you to seek out the Mexican who killed Stilson and his boys. He shouldn't be hard to find. There ain't many six-foot greasers around here. Check on that sheepherders' camp first.' He hard-eyed Ringold. 'And I want the sonuvabitch alive; he could be a member of a gang of Mexican *bandidos* though I don't think that's likely, but I need to know who the hell he is and why he offered to drive Farrow's wagon. I've got an uneasy feelin' in my gut it wasn't for what Farrow offered to pay him.'

* * *

'I'll raise a posse to rope in that Mexican, Saul,' Sheriff Smithson said, after he had given orders to his two deputies to take the bodies along to the undertaker's.

Farrow looked scathingly at the

lawman, belly overhanging his gunbelt with all the free beer he downed in the Long Branch. 'What the blazes do you want a posse for?' he said angrily. 'The dead fellas were the road agents who had been ambushing my supplies. The Mexican only did your job! If you want to raise a posse, well, lead them across to the saloon and ask Pearson how it comes that those fellas were on his payroll. But then you'll lose your free drinks and free humpings in the cat house!' Sheriff Smithson visibly winced as though he had been struck by a blow with a fist. Farrow gave him one last cutting look then turned and walked back into the store.

Sheriff Smithson began to sweat and curse Pearson for grabbing what he wanted too fast. He couldn't expect him as the town's law enforcer to look the other way when a senior citizen complained that he was having his supplies stolen. Now it seemed that as Farrow had forcibly told him, the Mexican had done his work for him.

Now came the hard part, he thought gloomily; he had to go across to the saloon and ask Pearson why was it that some of his men were taking up bushwhacking in their spare time. He damn well knew that the stealing of Farrow's supplies had been on Pearson's orders, but he had to make a show of acting as a vigilant lawman, or he would lose a lot of votes the next time he came up for re-election. He hoped to hell Pearson could lie his way out of this tight situation, or he would have to dish out free drinks in his bar again if he wanted him to do another stint as town sheriff.

Though he didn't pay for his drinks in the Long Branch, or his occasional all-nighters in the bawdy house, those activities weren't really free. The price was that he had to uphold the law in the territory, Pearson's law, such as harassing the small ranchers with restraining orders and fines if their cattle strayed on Pearson's grass. A regular occurrence on land that had no boundary fencing and would have been ignored by any other rancher but Pearson. Sheriff Smithson did some more dirty-mouthing. Jackson Pearson was one stomping man, a man who wanted to be big, fast. He knocked on Pearson's office door, but not before he'd had a shot of whiskey at the bar to boost up his courage. Rancher Pearson frightened him; he had the dead-eyed look of a man who had come by his wealth by other means than legal business deals.

He heard a grated-voiced, 'Come in!' and he pushed open the door and stepped inside. An Indian-faced Petch sat behind his big desk. Sheriff Smithson swallowed hard and sweated some more, and wished he'd had two whiskeys.

Looking more bold-assed than he was feeling he said, 'Things are gettin' hot across the street, Mr Pearson, what with Farrow findin' out that the bushwhackers — '

'I don't give a damn about what

Farrow suspects!' bellowed Petch, interrupting the sheriff. 'Tell him that I told you I paid them off weeks ago and they must be getting their wherewithal by thievin'! Your job is to find that Mex!'

'But he ain't broke any law, Mr Pearson,' the sheriff replied, trying to hold to what bit of integrity he had left as a lawman.

'The greaser sonuvabitch has gunned down three American boys!' Petch roared back, his face working in anger. 'And put back me gettin' hold of Farrow's store! Now git, and earn your free drinks and free women!' He gave the sheriff a final scowl and waved a dismissive hand.

Sheriff Smithson closed the door quietly behind him and walked to the bar with lots of frightening thoughts whirling around in his head. A Mexican *pistolero*, for some reason or other, was conducting a small war against Jackson Pearson and had drawn first blood, and he was being dragged into Pearson's private trouble. As he poured out a large shot of whiskey, with a hand that shook, he hoped that he wouldn't get to eyeballing the pistol of the deadly shooting greaser.

9

Farrow slept in a room above his store and had locked up before retiring for the night. He was feeling a whole heap happier than he had been at daybreak, though still puzzled about the non-appearance of his Mexican driver. In the morning, he promised himself, he would see about finding out where he lived and handing over the wages he owed him to his wife. A rapping at the rear door of the store stopped him at the foot of the stairs. Wondering who it could be this late at night he walked across to the door and opened it with the lantern held high. Two men were standing there, his missing driver, who, he could see with some surprise wasn't a Mexican at all, but as Yankee as he was. The short stocky-framed man with him was definitely a Mexican, and the ugliest Mexican he had ever clapped eyes on. The hand that held the lantern shook. The big American eased him back from the door and pushed past him, the Mexican following him in.

Sweet Jesus! Farrow thought wildly, the bastards had come to clean out his store! 'I've got your due ready, mister!' he said, the words as wild sounding as his thoughts. 'I was goin' to try and find — '

'Calm down, Mr Farrow,' interrupted Raynor. 'We mean you no harm. Sit down and put the lantern on the counter before you drop it and set fire to the store. We just want have a talk with you that's all.'

A limb-trembling Farrow did what he was told, still holding his gaze of the fierce-looking Mexican. A merciless gringo throat slitter if he ever saw one.

'Me and my *compadre*, Señor Santos,' Raynor began, 'have a long standin' dispute with a fella called Petch, a bank robber. You know him here in Gila Crossin' as Jackson Pearson, the *hombre*, I hear, who wants your store.'

Farrow rocked back in his chair. Pearson, a bank robber! Were his two late night callers joshing him? He could see no signs of humour on either of their hatchet-hewn faces. 'He — he said,' he stammered, 'that he came by his money by selling a silver mine he owned up north in Nevada to a big Eastern company.'

Raynor gave Farrow a hard-faced grin. 'The gold, Mr Farrow, came from a Texas bank, taken by the barrels of our guns. But the sonuvabitch double-crossed me and my pard, cut loose with all the takin's. Me and my pard are here to reclaim our share of the gold, and Petch's share as well. That's the reason I helped you. To get back at Petch, to cause him some grief until we can seize what cash he's got at his ranch and in the saloon and whorehouse here in town, *comprende?*'

Farrow nodded his head but remained silent. He was looking at two genuine killers. He knew for a fact they had killed three men. How many more had they gunned down in their bank-robbing days? And Pearson, Petch, whoever, had ridden with the pair. And he had stood up to Petch like one businessman to another. Farrow shuddered. How long would it have been before Petch concluded his dealings with him by shooting him dead if these two *pistoleros* hadn't shown up in Gila Crossing?

'Now we reckon that Petch will send out men to hunt down this tall 'Mexican' who drove your wagon so I will have to disappear,' Raynor said. 'Yet I need to stay close enough to town so I can keep an eye on Petch, not too close for him to recognize me though. So what I want to ask you is, can you recollect anyone hereabouts who hates Petch's guts enough to let me hide out on his place?'

Santos spoke for the first time in a voice as intimidating as his look. 'My *amigo* is trusting you, gringo. If you tell Petch of our being here he will kill you because he will know that you know he is a robber of banks, a *bandido*. If by some chance he lets you live then I will kill you for betraying us.'

Santos's devil-like smile froze Farrow's throat muscles. His lips moved several times but no words came out. Finally he got enough control of his nerves to say, 'There's Jonas Curry, owns a farm just outa town, Petch's puttin' the pressure on him to sell him his holdin'.'

'We met him on the way here,' Raynor said. 'It would be too risky for him and his family for me to hole-up on his place. Petch will check first on all the men he's upset thinkin' that they could have hired a Mexican *pistolero* to fight him off.' He grinned, and Farrow thought his smile was every bit as throat gagging as his Mexican partner's was. 'He'll wonder if you could have done the hirin'.'

'To hell with Petch!' Farrow said bold-voiced, feeling suddenly some of the true grit his pioneering grandpappy had. 'He can think what he goddamn likes!' He managed a smile of sorts. 'He might stop harassin' me if he reckons I've hired a genuine *pistolero*. But gettin' back to your question, mister, about findin' a place to hole-up, I figure Mr Lassiter will be more than pleased to give you shelter.'

'Who's this Lassiter?' Raynor asked.

'An Easterner, a hard man from Chicago,' Farrow replied. 'He used to own the Long Branch saloon and the whorehouse until Petch came on the scene. He wanted to buy him out. Lassiter told him to tend to his cows and keep his nose out of his business. A week later, Lassiter was bushwhacked by fellas the sheriff ain't yet roped in, and can only get about now with the help of a coupla sticks. He was forced to sell the saloon and bawdy house to Petch, at the sonuvabitch's price, to pay his doctor's bills. Any enemy of Petch will be like a long lost brother to Lassiter, I reckon.'

'It will be worth payin' this Lassiter a visit, Santos,' Raynor said. Then he asked the storekeeper where the cripple lived.

'Just on the outskirts of the town,' Farrow said. 'On the north trail. You can't miss his place, it's a big adobe built house facin' the creek. Lassiter has no kin livin' with him, only a Mexican woman who cooks and cleans for him.' Farrow smiled again. 'Petch passes the house every time he comes into town; he'll never guess that you'll be that close to him.'

'Thank you for your help, Mr Farrow,' Raynor replied. 'Now, if you hand over what you owe me for bringin' your stores in, me and my pard will be on our way and let you get to bed.'

Some hope of sleep, Farrow thought gloomily, as he handed over a roll of bills, more than he had intended to pay, to the big man. Not when three hard men were about to settle their differences with guns. Innocent bystanders had been shot dead in suchlike bloody situations. And he could be one of them.

After they left the store, Raynor and Santos split up, Santos to ride back to the sheepherders' camp, Raynor, not willing to take any risks, rode out of town to spend the rest of the night wrapped up in his blanket in a fireless camp, though warmed with the comforting thought that they had struck the first hard blow against Petch.

Next day, he waited until mid-morning and made sure the trail was clear, before riding the short distance to the fine built house bordering the creek.

The man who answered to his knock seemed only as old as he was, yet his hair was white, his face deeply etched by long-time pain lines and he was leaning heavily on two sticks. He scowled up at Raynor. 'I don't give handouts to saddle bums!' he snarled. 'Scram!'

Raynor gave him a quick assaying glance. He had seen that stone-eyed look before, every time he looked in a mirror. Farrow spoke of Lassiter as a hard man from Chicago. He didn't know if lawbreakers in the Eastern city were called owlhoots, or outlaws, but he was gazing on a man who had taken what he wanted by force and threats; a man who would reason like him, or so he was about to gamble on, as he came to a quick decision.

'Mr Lassiter,' he said. 'I've hard-assed it all the way from Mexico to kill a no-good sonuvabitch called Petch; you know him as Jackson Pearson and I know that you reckon he had something to do with the way you are now. I'd be obliged if you would help me out. If you ain't in a helpin' mood then I'll be on my way and apologize for disturbin' you.' He stood and waited for Lassiter's reaction.

Lassiter did some rapid weighing up of his own. He had played cards, clinched shady deals with cheats, lying men, blowhards and stone-faced back-stabbers and had developed a talent for judging the characters of men behind all their mouthing The big man meant what he had said.

He opened the door wider. 'Come inside, mister,' he said. 'And tell me more of this joyous news over a glass of whiskey.'

Raynor relaxed. He grinned at Lassiter. 'Make that whiskey, coffee, Mr Lassiter and I'd welcome sittin' at your table, jawin' about Mr Jackson Pearson.'

Raynor sat in a big upholstered chair as easy on his back and ass as any bed he had slept in. Lassiter sat opposite him in a similar high-backed chair. On a small table close by him was a glass and a half-filled bottle of Irish whiskey. It seemed, Raynor thought, that Mr Lassiter started his drinking real early in the day, by his drawn-faced look, to ease his pain. He was drinking a cup of coffee made for him by a plump, elderly Mexican woman who smiled slightly at him when he thanked her in her own language. With a 'Gracias, señor,' she left to go back into the kitchen.

'Now tell me the reason that brought you up here from Mexico to kill this

94

fella with two names,' Lassiter said. 'Though if I could stand steady enough to hold a gun, you would have made your trip for nothing, mister, because I would have put paid to the bastard myself, even if it was in the middle of Main Street, and the law could hang me with pleasure.'

'Then it was definitely Petch who crippled you?' Raynor said.

Lassiter gave a thin, painful laugh. 'Oh, Petch hired the bushwhacker who crippled me all right. He wanted to buy me out, but I turned him down. Then he did what I would have done if I'd wanted to buy his ranch and he didn't want to sell. Though I would have killed the sonuvabitch, not leave him half a man.'

He held his cold-eyed stare on Raynor as if daring him to deny his statement before reaching for his glass and taking a deep swallow of the pain-killing liquor.

'Petch gave orders to gun me down, mister,' he repeated, more to himself than his visitor. 'I hail from Chicago where I ran a gambling joint before I came here and bought the saloon and the cat house. I've played poker with men who would make your *pistoleros*, owlhoots, whatever, look like altar boys. Those boys operated the same way as Petch did to take control of some other fella's well-paying business, kill him or burn him out! Now tell me why you are risking a hanging to get even with Mr Petch.'

Raynor began telling Lassiter who he was, then went on to relate the events after the successful bank raid at Grantsburg. How Petch had double-crossed the gang and shot down Hardropp and Baxter and the wounding of him and Santos so that he could ride off with all of the bank's takings.

'Later, I took up with a bunch of Missourian hard men and did some raidin' in the Nations,' he continued. 'It was there that I heard that Petch, now callin' himself Pearson, was makin' it big in Gila Crossin' on money that should have been split five ways. I rode down to Mexico and contacted my old *amigo*, José Santos, a genuine Mexican *bandido*.' He grinned across at Lassiter. 'No offence to the tough *hombres* in Chicago you spoke of, Mr Lassiter, but Santos in a bad mood is one *mal hombre*, a real bad-ass, and would send your toughs scatterin' for their hole-ups. I knew he would want to be in at the kill, so here we are after all this time, within pistol range of the sonuvabitch who left us for dead. Santos wanted to blow off Petch's head pronto-like, but I told him that wouldn't get us our money back, only a hemp collar each if we didn't hightail it back across the border.'

'This Petch gunned down his own boys!' Lassiter shook his head in disbelief. 'Gangs fought gangs in Chicago over gambling rights in some district or other, but they were loyal to their own gang members. I can understand you wanting to kill Petch, but how do you reckon on getting your hands on Petch's money? He keeps it close by him. If you're thinking of robbing the safe at the ranch house, forget it. Petch has a crew of at least twenty men; you'll never get within five miles of the house.'

Raynor favoured Lassiter with another cold-faced grin. 'We'll take what cash there is in the saloon and whorehouse then burn them down. We want to hurt Petch where it'll hurt him most, takin' his cash, before we figure out a way to kill him without danger to ourselves.'

Then Raynor told Lassiter about posing as a Mexican and his and Santos's killing of three of Petch's men when they tried to bushwhack the wagon, preventing Petch from taking over Farrow's stores. 'And that's the reason I'm payin' a call on you, Mr Lassiter. Petch will have set up a hunt for the big Mexican who put paid to his plans and killed his men, so I have to go back to bein' a tall gringo. That means I can't show myself in Gila Crossin' in case I bump into Petch, because then the sonuvabitch will fort-up in his big house and me and Santos will never get a shot at him, or any of our money back. Santos is OK, he's stayin' with the Mexican sheepherders on the edge of town. I need a good place to hole-up until I reckon it's safe to go into town and check out the saloon and whorehouse before we rob them. I'd be rightly obliged if you could let me stay in one of your outbuildin's until I'm ready to make my move.'

'You can stay here in the house, Mr Raynor,' Lassiter said, without any hesitation.

'Thanks for your offer, Mr Lassiter,' replied Raynor. 'But I'm an old owlhoot and can only rest my head where I know I've got a fast way out of any possible trouble. Shut up behind four walls, well . . . I would never rest.'

'There's a woodshed at the rear of the house large enough for you and your horse,' Lassiter said, 'Señora Luis will give you blankets and see that you are well fed. There's a well-hidden but passable horse trail beyond the shed that leads to broken up country where a man could lie low. And there'll be no risk for you when you ride into town. Petch, whenever he rides into Gila, crosses the creek by the ford; likewise when he rides back to his ranch. Petch is in town now. I pass most of my days sitting at that big window which overlooks the ford so when the bastard heads back to his ranch I can let you know.'

Things were turning out real well for him and Santos, Raynor thought. They had a good ally in their fight against Petch. Information when Petch was, or was not, in town was vital. Even Santos would be pleased the way the cards were being dealt in their favour. He came quickly out of his thoughts as he heard Lassiter say, 'I reckon it would be of some interest to a safe cracker if he knew exactly where the safes he was reckoning on robbing were located in the buildings he couldn't suss out without drawing unwanted attention on himself.'

'It would save this heister a lot of dangerous nosin' around, Mr Lassiter,' Raynor replied. 'Nosiness is one of the fastest ways to get a man killed.'

'The safe in the whorehouse is in the madame's room, a part Mex female, on the first floor facing Main Street. When she isn't with Petch she's making sure her girls are keeping the gamblers happy. The one in the saloon is in Petch's private room at the rear of the bar.' Lassiter's face twisted in a grimace of a grin. 'I had the keys to them once.'

'Mr Lassiter,' Raynor said. 'You've given me an edge over Petch. I can see Santos and me headin' back to Mexico a helluva lot richer and Petch dead longways before I thought we would.' He got to his feet. 'I thank you for your hospitality, *amigo*, and your help. I'll swing wide of Gila Crossin' to the Mex camp and let my pard know I've got a place to lie low and arrange regular rendezvous with him so once you tell me that Petch has left town we can start openin' his safes.'

'You do that,' Lassiter replied. 'It's been a pleasure meeting you. When I hear of Petch's death it will cheer me up no end.'

As Raynor opened the door he called out, 'One thing more, Mr Raynor, I've heard that your old gang boss deals in stolen cattle.'

Raynor turned round to face Lassiter. 'That's a new line for Petch,' he said in a surprised voice. 'We never lifted cattle when we rode as a gang.'

'That's m'be so,' Lassiter said. 'I reckon you didn't stay in one place long enough to run cattle. But Petch is a rancher now and his herd is growing fast. According to one of the working girls in the whorehouse, when I still owned it, this fella Ringold, who once rode with a bunch of rustlers up there around Tombstone, told her, when he had been hitting the bottle, that he had just come up from below the border with a bunch of stolen greaser cattle, his word not mine, and had sold them to a big rancher in the territory. Now your guess is as good as mine who that rancher is, Mr Raynor?'

Raynor let out a low whistle. 'Well, I'll be damned. Me and Santos hit the bastard harder than we thought.' He then told Lassiter of the shooting down of the cattle-stealers in Sonora and the scattering of the herd. 'It'll not be long before Petch links up the two shootin's and he'll be as mad as hell, drive his men hard to find that tall 'Mexican'. One thing's for sure: he'll hang fire tryin' to grab hold of some other fella's land or property until he's sorted out who's killin' his men.'

Raynor made the wide circle around Gila Crossing undetected, thinking that him and Santos were driving Petch into a corner. Robbing then burning down his saloon and bawdy house would have him backing right up to the wall.

10

It was late afternoon the day after his meeting with Pearson before Ringegold, backed by two men, Josh Cassidy and Billy Jenson, made it to the Mexican sheepherders' camp. The pair had been playing in an all day poker game and Ringegold had to wait until their run of good luck had turned sour and they had slept off all the liquor they had downed at the card table. But he reckoned the wait had been worth it. Ringegold fancied himself as a hard man: he had stolen cattle, robbed wagon-trains riding with the Clanton gang, men who would kill a man if they didn't like the way he looked at them, but he wasn't foolhardy. He had more than a gut feeling that the Mexican wasn't working on his own and he didn't want to get caught short like Pearson's three boys must have been.

Cassidy and Jenson, though the bastards had had him kicking heels for twenty-four hours, had well-deserved reps as men who could use a pistol or a long gun with speed and deadly effect against anyone they were paid to shoot down.

He had sent out the two men left of his cattle-stealing gang to ask the sodbusters along Gila Creek if they had seen a tall Mexican riding across their land. He wasn't expecting them to be told of any sightings of the Mexican Pearson wanted, but he was the man footing the bill so he had to go through the motions that he was doing a widespread search.

It was siesta time and the sheep were milling about unattended, their herders lying corpse-like under the sun break of a stand of timber. In the camp itself even the sun had driven the children inside their ramshackle homes or under crude tarp lean-tos.

'Get down off your horse, Billy,' Ringold said, 'And wake up that greaser and ask him if that fella we're lookin' for is stayin' in the camp.'

Billy swung down from his saddle and walked the few paces to the Mexican sitting with his back up against a shaded wall of a hut wrapped in his *serape* with his sombrero tilted over his face. He nudged him sharply in the ribs with the toe of his boot.

'Hey, greaser, wake up!' he said. 'I want to ask you a few questions.'

Santos lifted his head slightly and Billy Jenson glimpsed eyes as hard and cold as a sidewinder's. Involuntarily he stepped back a pace, hand dropping to his pistol butt.

'Pilgrim,' Raynor breathed, bellied down behind a ridge, 'you don't know how close you're standin' to the Grim Reaper.' He had come on to the camp from across the creek just in time to catch sight of the three riders entering the camp from the main trail out of Gila Crossing. He drew out his rifle and dismounted and dropped to the ground from where he could cover Santos if things got out of hand. He hoped that his *compadre* would rein in his hair-trigger temper, or the sheriff would be riding into the camp looking for the men who had gunned down three gringos. To escape a hanging they would have to asskick it back to Mexico and their grand plan to get even with Petch would be over just when it was beginning to work.

'*No entiende inglés,*' Santos growled, his pistol cocked beneath his serape, ready to shoot the gringo in the groin if he kicked him again.

Billy turned and looked up at Ringold. 'I can't make any sense of what the bastard spouted; he don't seem to understand good American lingo.'

'OK, let him sleep,' Ringold replied. 'We're wastin' our time here, Billy. If that Mex was smart enough to get the better of three armed men then he'll be smart enough to have found himself a good hide-out.'

'We could drag a kid outa one of

those rat-hole shacks,' Cass butted in. 'Ask him if he's seen a tall Mexican hangin' around the camp. Threaten to beat the crap outa him if he don't talk.'

Ringold gave him a fish-eyed look. 'Don't let those greasers lyin' on the ground fool you, Cass. Lay a hand on one of their brats and they'll be on us cuttin' with their machetes. I know, I've fought against them. When their blood is up the sonsuvbitches are as crazy mean as any Injun. Let's move out; we've done what Pearson wanted us to, and checked out the sheepherders' camp.'

'But where do we look next for the Mex, Ringold?' asked Billy. 'We can't hope to find him out there.' He pointed with his chin at the long line of jagged peaks ahead of them. 'A whole goddamned army could go to ground up there and not one of them would be spotted.'

'We go back to town,' Ringold said. 'And stay alert to wait for the Mex's next move in his dispute with Pearson.

If we're quick off the mark we could m'be pick up his trail before he gets holed-up in the high ground.'

Raynor breathed a deep sigh of relief as he watched the three ride out, opining that the sharp-featured man who had been giving out the orders must be Ringold, the hired gun Lassiter told him about, the boss man of the gang of cattle-lifters he and Santos had shot down. Raynor's face hardened in grim lines. If he stood in his way to get at Petch then Mr Ringold would end up just as dead as his boys back there in Sonora.

He came down from the ridge and met up with Santos, who was on his feet and gazing with hate-filled eyes at the receding cloud of trail dust.

Raynor grinned, 'Don't fret any, *amigo*,' he said. 'We'll choose our own ground to get them outa our hair. Though we've already started doin' that. The fella who did the most talkin' was the boss of that cattle-liftin' bunch we ambushed. It's only been a week or so since we rode out of Casa Grande and we've put paid to nine of Petch's hired guns. The way the sonuvabitch has got men lookin' for me shows that he's feelin' the heat. I figure we oughta keep the flames flarin'. Get saddled up and I'll introduce you to Mr Lassiter, another fella who would be mighty pleased to see Petch dead. He's keepin' a look-out for when Petch rides back to his ranch. When he does we'll make a trip into Gila Crossin' and see if we can come up with a plan on how to get hold of the cash in those two safes' — he wolf-grinned — 'and m'be take out some more of Petch's bully boys, to kinda impress on them that workin' for Mr Pearson ain't like gettin' money from home: it could get them an early plot on Boot Hill.'

★ ★ ★

Lassiter, on seeing Santos, had to agree with what Raynor had told him. The Mexican, even in a happy mood, would throw a scare in most men. He became confident that being he was cripple, he couldn't dance on Petch's grave, but as sure as hell he would enjoy relieving himself on it.

'Good news, Mr Raynor,' he said. 'Petch is on his way back to his ranch. He crossed the creek about an hour ago. I don't know what you plan to do but you and your pard are welcome to stay here until you're ready to make your move against Petch. There's food ready if you want to eat.'

'Me and Santos wouldn't turn down the chance of some fine cooked chow, Mr Lassister,' Raynor said. 'After we've eaten it should be dark enough for us to sneak into Gila Crossin' and check things out. I think we'll take the saloon's cash first, if that sits well with you, *amigo*?'

The *amigo* grinned. An expression that raised the hair on the back of Lassiter's neck.

*   *   *

Lassiter made it to the porch to see Raynor and Santos mount up and ride out then he returned to his big chair by the fire, and the bottle of whiskey, buoyed up by pleasant thoughts of the kinds of hell his two visitors were about to inflict on the man who had him crippled.

11

Raynor strode casually into the Long Branch saloon, though by force of habit his gaze flickered which way and every way, hand hovering close to the butt of his pistol. He stood just left of the door for a moment or two to take in the scene before carrying on to the bar. The place was crowded with drinkers, well into their loud-mouthed, back-slapping state of drunkenness. He caught sight of the two gunmen who had been with Rinegold at the sheepherders' camp at a table playing poker with two other men. By the pair's scowling looks the cards didn't seem to be running in their favour. Santos, who had ridden into town twenty minutes earlier, was standing with his back against the bar eyeing the players, doing some fierce scowling of his own. Raynor's lips twitched in a ghost of a grin. You may think that you've hit a streak of bad luck, pilgrims, he thought, but, by hell, real crappy luck's heading your way soon. He bellied up to the bar next to Santos.

'I've seen the sonsuvbitches, *amigo*,' he said softly, as he gazed at his reflection in the bar mirror, 'but we'll pass the time of day with them later. First things first, like gettin' hold of all the cash those tills are ringin' up once it gets locked up in the saloon's safe. I reckon that door at the far end of the bar leads to the office.'

Santos, still dead-eying the two gunmen, only gave a grunt in reply.

'We can't blow the safe, José,' Raynor continued. 'I noticed a coupla shotgun-armed deputies patrollin' Main Street; they'll be on to us before the safe door's swung open. Somehow we have to persuade the manager of this gin palace to open it after he locks up the saloon for the night. I reckon that fella wearin' the fancy vest talkin' to that redhead is the manager.' He paused and caught the attention of one of the overworked barkeeps and indicated he wanted a beer. Before he had been served he said. almost as an afterthought, 'Most *hombres* can be persuaded to do a thing they're against doin' if a .44 Colt pistol is pressed against their heads, Santos.'

'We could blow up the bank, *compadre*,' Santos said, turning round to meet Raynor's surprised gaze in the bar mirror. 'Not the safe, the bank. Heave a couple of sticks of dynamite through one of the windows and you'll have all of Gila Crossing out on the street and leave it clear for you to grab hold of that fancy dressed *hombre* and do your persuading.'

Raynor took a pull of the glass of beer the barkeep had put down in front of him as he considered Santos's suggestion.

'Yeah, that could work, *compadre*,' he said. 'M'be you could cut loose with a few pistol shells to kinda fool them that the no-good bank robbers are still inside the bank, make the sheriff and his deputies a mite wary rushin' in there. That oughta win me some extra time to make that fella over there open up his safe.' He cast a sidelong glance at Santos. 'Providin' you don't blow the goddamned bank to smithereens.' Raynor finished off his beer in one long quick swallow. 'Finish your drink off, *amigo*, and let's pay a call on our friend Mr Farrow. He's sure to have some spare sticks of dynamite in his store.'

★　★　★

The first indication that Farrow knew he had unwelcome visitors was when he had been shaken roughly awake. His first sleep-fogged thought was that he was dreaming. The store was all locked up but the heavy hand on his shoulder felt real enough. He jerked upright in his bed, clear visioned. By the flickering light of the bedside lantern he saw his ex-wagon driver and his bowel-loosening Mexican partner standing

116

alongside his bed. Farrow's nerves twanged painfully with the sudden shock.

'We apologize for waking you up, Mr Farrow,' from the tall Texan eased a little of his fears. Enough for him to croak, 'How . . . how did you get in? I locked all the doors.'

Raynor grinned down at him pityingly. 'It would pay you to have stronger locks fitted, Mr Farrow. Why, if me and my pard were a coupla penny-ante thieves we could have cleaned out all your stores without you knowin' it. Now what we are here for is to ask you if you've got any sticks of blastin' powder in your store. A coupla sticks will do.'

'Blastin' powder!' Farrow almost leaped out of his bed. 'Blastin' powder!' he repeated, his voice as high-pitched as a young girl's 'What for?'

'We are going to blow up the bank, señor,' a grinning Santos said.

Farrow opined that if he was destined for hell when his time came he would be greeted with a more honest smile from the Devil than the fiercely twisted apology for one with which the Mexican was favouring him. He swallowed hard. He was, against his will, about to be an accomplice in blowing up the town's bank. He lacked the backbone to tell the murderous pair he wanted no part in suchlike illegal activity in case the Mexican slashed his throat with his fearsome-looking machete. Instead, he said, his throat drying up again, 'There's a box of dynamite somewhere in the back of the store. Farmers use it to blast out deep-rooted tree stumps.'

'Good,' replied Raynor. 'Now you just get your head back on that pillow and go back to sleep; we'll find that box.' Raynor grinned. 'Then if the sheriff comes in enquirin' where the dynamite came from that blew up the bank you can look him in the eye and say that some no-good thieves broke into the store while you were asleep and stole some sticks of blastin' powder. You can show him the broken lock on the door and the levered open box of fire crackers.'

Blow up the bank! Farrow thought wildly. And the big stone-faced bastard wanted him to go back to sleep as though nothing was going to happen!

He lay awake until he could no longer hear the scraping of crates being moved around, then he was out of bed and, with a blanket draped over his shoulders, he hauled a chair to a window which gave him a clear view of the bank. Any action that would hurt Petch was worth losing a few hours' sleep. Though he did wonder how blowing up the bank would upset the rancher; the son-of-a-bitch kept his money in a safe in the ranch's big house. He could only wait and see. His villainous-looking night callers didn't seem men who blew up buildings just for the hell of it.

12

'It will be daylight in four, five hours, *amigo*,' Santos growled impatiently. 'And those gringo dogs are still drinking.'

Raynor and Santos were at the end of a blind side alley facing the Long Branch saloon waiting for it to close so that they could get their hands on the contents of the saloon's safe.

Raynor grinned in the dark. 'Don't be mean-assed, *compadre*,' he said. 'Those poor bastards drinkin' in that gin palace tend ornery, stinkin' cows for a livin'; they're entitled to whoop it up when payday comes round.' Though he was as eager as Santos to get things rolling. The shotgun deputies were still patrolling along Main Street and there was an ever present danger of them spotting two suspicious characters lurking in the alley and that could bring shooting trouble on him and Santos.

Finally, to their relief, they saw the last of the well-liquored up cow hands being helped into his saddle by some of his less drunken buddies. Though it was not until the last high-spirited whoops and wild pistol discharges from the departing ranch hands had long since faded away that the pair saw four saloon girls come out of the bar and head along Main Street chatting to one another. Raynor surmised that they would be making for their rooming-house. A few minutes later, an elderly man stepped out on to the porch and Raynor recognized him as the saloon's swamper. After blowing out the flames on the two lanterns that hung either side of the swing doors, leaving the saloon in total darkness, he walked along the street in the same direction that the dance girls had taken. Now only the manager would be in there, Raynor opined. He grinned. Which would be no problem to a professional bank robber. Even if he locked himself in his room, Santos's handiwork would have him rushing out to see what all the noise was about, right on to his pistol barrel, Raynor thought confidently.

Raynor sensed rather than saw Santos move; he put a restraining hand on his shoulder and nodded towards the open end of the alley. 'Let those sonsuvbitches pass first,' he whispered. And Santos saw the faint shapes of the two deputies walking along the far side of Main Street. Then came a few tense minutes' waiting until they judged the deputies were well along the street.

'OK, let's open up the ball, *amigo*,' Raynor said. 'But we'll circle the saloon first to check out that the manager has gone to bed, that he ain't sittin' up workin' on his accounts by lamplight.'

They met up under the darker shadows of the saloon's porch, pistols fisted, leaving nothing to chance.

'All in darkness, Juan,' Santos said.

'Likewise my side,' replied Raynor. 'Give me five minutes to get inside then you alter the shape of that bank.'

It didn't take long for an expert thief to break the lock on the rear door of the saloon and step inside a long dark passage. Raynor stood still for a moment or two to get his eyes used to the deeper darkness of the inside of the saloon. At the far end of the passage he saw a strip of light at the foot of a door. There was a chance Raynor thought, that he could grab hold of the saloon manager before the explosions had him haring out of his room. Cat-footed he walked along the passage to the door and quietly tried the handle. The door was locked. Then he heard voices on the other side of the door, one of them a female's. Raynor did some low-voiced cursing: the horn dog manager had a woman with him.

Raynor would suffer no pangs of conscience if he had to shoot the manager to get into the safe, but he had never shot a female before. Santos, he knew, would not hesitate in shooting her if she got in the way. He was just debating with himself whether or not to call off the raid when the dynamite exploded. The shockwaves shook the foundations of the saloon and showered him with the dust of ages from the walls and the ceiling of the passageway.

Raynor heard the key click in the lock and the door swung open and the saloon manager, wearing only his drawers stood framed in the door. Over his shoulder, by the light of a fancy lamp resting on a table, Raynor caught a tantalizing glimpse of a dark-haired girl lying on the bed and by what he could see of her she was jaybird naked.

Jason Amiss, the saloon manager, gasped in surprise and alarm on seeing a tall Mexican standing outside his door. His wondering how and why the son-of-a-bitch had got into the saloon was cut off short, and painfully, as a pistol was pushed sharply under his nose. Fear rapidly cooled the lust the brunette had been raising in him. He had heard of the tall Mexican, the killer of three of his once regular customers; he was still the main topic of conversation in the bar. And now the killing *pistolero* was here!

Raynor spoke to the girl first, as scared-faced as her boss, now covering up her nakedness with a sheet. '*Señorita*,' he said with a heavy Mexican accent, 'you stay nice and quiet and you'll come to no harm. If you scream then I'll have to kill you, *comprende*?' His mad-eyed scowl would have earned him praise from Santos. The girl nodded dumbly. Then he eyeballed the manager. 'You, *señor*,' he grated 'are goin' to open that safe of yours for me. Any funny business and I'll kill you both.' Raynor cast another fearsome look at the girl. 'And I don't reckon you'll want that pretty, hot-blooded *señorita*'s death on your conscience.'

'I'll get the keys,' a tight-throated Amiss croaked. 'They're in the drawer of that table at the head of the bed.'

'Go and get them, then,' Raynor ordered.

Amiss heard the ominous click of a pistol hammer being thumbed back behind him as he walked the few steps to the table. There was also a fully loaded pistol in the drawer, but he wasn't foolish enough to make a grab for it. That such a mad-ass trick could get the girl killed didn't worry him at all, but it would sure as hell get him dead, and his staying alive was all that mattered. The greaser son-of-a-bitch could have the money in the safe, it was only a few hundred dollars — Pearson's dollars.

Raynor kept a watchful gaze on the saloon manager as he opened the drawer. If there was a pistol in that drawer, and by the glint he had caught in the manager's eyes he guessed there was, he didn't think he had the balls to risk a shoot-out with him. Though he also knew that sometimes when pressed tight between a rock and a hard place, the most unlikely of men find a spark of retaliatory courage. Then Raynor would find out if he had the balls to shoot down a woman.

The tension eased out of Raynor

when the manager turned and all he held in his hand was a ring of keys. 'Let's go and open that safe, *señor*,' he said. 'And you stay just as quiet as you are now, *señorita*, and no harm will come to you.' As he shepherded the manager along the passage to the room that held the safe, Raynor heard the sound of gunshots — one gun; Santos was stirring up the pot.

The two deputies doing the night shift were sharing a pot of coffee with the sheriff in his office when the twin explosions shattered the calm of the night, and all the windows along Main Street.

'Holy Moses!' a wild-eyed Sheriff Smithson gasped. 'That sounds as though it came from the bank!'

There was a scattering of mugs and upending of chairs as the three lawmen made a dash for the door, the sheriff pausing only long enough to grab a rifle from the rack and throw a bandolier of reloads across his shoulder. Their boots crunching window glass beneath their feet, they ran along the board-walk to the bank now partly hidden by a high rising pall of dust.

Santos cut loose at the two deputies, tumbling them down howling with pain from their shattered knees. Sheriff Smithson hit the dirt fast, cursing like a muleskinner. He heard his deputies groaning in agony so at least they were still alive. Quickly he began to weigh up the situation. By the sound of the two explosions, the bank-raiders must have used too much dynamite to blow open the safe and had somehow got themselves trapped inside. Why else would the bastards still be in the building when they must know that the whole damn town, and beyond, had heard the racket, alerting them that their bank was being robbed.

The sheriff risked raising his head slightly, the dust was clearing slowly enough for him to notice that the bank's front adobe wall was lying shattered in Main Street, which supported his theory that the robbers, in their foolish handling of the dynamite, had sprung a trap for themselves.

He saw lantern-light shine out of the opening door of the funeral parlour and yelled out, 'Don't step out, Mr Murphy, the bank's being raided and some of them are still inside. They've wounded Sal and Larry! Go out by the back door and round up a posse. There's a chance we can ring the bastards in until daylight. Then we can have us a turkey shoot.'

The lamp on the big desk in the office had been lit and Amiss was on his knees fumbling nervously for the right key on the ring. Raynor stood over him, his pistol only inches from his head. Even if there had been windows in the office, Raynor thought, the night deputies would have taken no heed of lights showing so early in the saloon's premises. Lanterns would be lit in every building along Main Street. It was not every night the townsfolk got the excitement of having their bank blown up.

Eventually, Amiss managed to open the safe and Raynor saw the money bags of coins and the small bundles of paper dollars lying on the top shelf. Amiss got to his feet, his usefulness was over and Raynor brought his Colt down hard on the manager's head. Amiss groaned and dropped to the floor in a crumpled heap. Raynor grabbed the money bags and wads of cash and stuffed them into the knapsack he had brought with him. Then he quickly stepped back into the passage. The light from the office lamp partly lit up the dark passage and Raynor caught a glimpse of a figure standing just inside the rear doorway, his gun came up. Then he heard Santos's growl, 'Is that you, *amigo*?'

'Yeah,' replied Raynor and he eased the hammer of the Colt forward. 'Everything's gone smoothly, so let's get to hell outa town before we have to fight our way through the crush eyeballin' what you've left left standin' of the bank.'

As they were sneaking their way to their horses, a man hurrying past them called out, 'Are you boys joinin' the picket line round the bank the sheriff's settin' up? He's hopin' to box in that bunch of bank robbers, or those that the blastin' powder ain't blew to bits!'

'We sure are, friend,' replied Raynor. 'We're just goin' for our long guns. We've heard those fellas trapped in the bank are a mean bunch of killers and bank heisters. We're not reckonin' on gettin' too close to those *mal hombres*. Shootin' them down at long range suits me and my pard.'

They heard the man laugh and say, 'That's why I've brung my pappy's old .50 calibre Sharps. This old buffalo gun can clear them outa their saddles as far away as the county line.'

* * *

Lassiter was standing on the porch when Raynor drew up his horse and dismounted. Santos had returned to the

131

sheepherders' camp to pass himself as a sheep man again if any of Petch's men came snooping around once more, searching for the tall 'Mexican'.

'I heard the bangs from here, Mr Raynor,' Lassiter said, when Raynor stepped on to the porch alongside him. 'And by your smirk I figure that you and your hard-face partner have got the saloon's takings.'

'We have that, Mr Lassiter,' replied Raynor. 'Petch will be hearin' some more bad news soon. We'll wait for a coupla days or so for the town to quieten down then we'll hurt Petch some more. Rob his cat house, then put a torch to it and the saloon. That oughta have Petch runnin' round like a headless chicken wonderin' who the hell's causin' him sleepless nights. And that could give me and Santos the chance to sneak into his big house and surprise him real good. Then we'll shoot him and take what cash he must have stashed away in there.' He grinned at Lassiter. 'Then our bank-robbin' days should be over. We can buy ourselves a parcel of grassland and raise a herd of beef.'

In spite of his constant pain, Lassiter managed a genuine broad-faced grin. 'You and your pard have set yourself a busy few days, Mr Raynor,' he said, though reasoning as a gambling man that the big Texan and his Mex pard were risking their necks on a hell of a lot of good luck coming their way. He kept that thought to himself, saying instead, 'Come inside and have a drink before you bed down for the night.'

'Once I've seen to my horse,' Raynor replied, 'I'd welcome a glass of your fine whiskey.' He grinned at Lassiter. 'My *amigo* will have to make do with home-stilled rotgut tequila. He'll shoot lumps out of me if he finds I've been partakin' of drinkin' quality liquor.'

* * *

The sun was well up when a shirtless Raynor came out of the barn to wash himself at the water trough. Sun dried, he walked back into the barn and finished dressing then made his way across to the house. With his belted Colt and carrying his rifle he felt uncomfortable being asked to sit down at a table with fine china laid on a clean white cloth.

As he stepped through the rear door he could smell bacon frying and the strong tangy aroma of freshly brewed coffee. And he began to wonder what the hell he and Santos and the rest of the gang had got out of all the banks and stage heists they had carried out. They had been eating and sleeping like a pack of mangy dogs since they had took up being owlhoots. When they had got a good haul it would be blown in some dog-dirt backwoods town on whiskey and lewd women a respectable Indian would pass by. Maybe, he thought, when they got hold of Petch's stash and bought their ranch they could hire a female Mex cook, like Lassiter's, to fix his and Santos's meals, served on proper plates, not battered, smoke-blackened tin ones.

Lassiter was sitting in his chair by the window overlooking the creek. He smiled up at Raynor. 'Before you eat I reckon you'd like to know that Petch is back in Gila Crossing. He crossed the creek not more than a half-hour ago, in one helluva hurry. Had four of his crew riding with him. I've never seen him come into town with an escort before. You must be worrying him.'

Raynor grinned. 'Me and Santos have hard-assed it all the way up from Sonora to do just that. And he's got some more frettin' to do before the final showdown, Mr Lassiter. I'm meetin' up with Santos later on and depending on what Petch is orderin' his bully boys to do, we'll plan our own moves.'

'I'd plan well then, Mr Raynor,' Lassiter said soberly. 'Petch has some hard men on his payroll. And tough men like Rinegold who don't officially work for him.' His face hardened, 'But

135

who the hell am I to tell you how to conduct your affairs? I allowed Petch to catch me off guard. Now go and get your breakfast; the *señora* don't like the chow she's cooked getting cold.'

'Don't worry yourself about me and Santos's well-bein', Mr Lassiter,' Raynor replied. 'We know that sonuvabitch, Petch. Christ, we rode together, killed and robbed together, farted together for years. Petch got the better of me and Santos once. He failed to kill us; a mistake that's goin' to get him an early grave.' He smiled at Lassiter. 'Now I'd better go and please the *señora* by eatin' that fine chow I can smell bein' cooked.'

13

Ringegold, though he didn't know it, was seeing Petch, the bank robber, in the man he knew as Mr Pearson. Pearson was no longer the oily-smiling, big shot rancher, a man with his sights on a position in the state government. To Ringegold he had the crazy-eyed look of old man Clanton, the patriach of a family of cattle thieves operating around Tombstone, as he stomped to and fro behind his desk. That led Ringegold to think that Pearson hadn't made his money by selling a silver mine. The bastard was an ex-owlhoot and came by his pile by law-breaking means.

Petch stopped his pacing and dropped down on his chair. He glared up at Ringegold. 'Find that Mex!' he said. The mad look in his eyes had died down somewhat, but his anger was still visibly showing by the nervous tic pulsating on his right cheek. 'Double check that Mex sheepherders' camp. Take a greaser with you to do the questionin' in their own lingo.' The madness came raging in his eyes again. 'Force one of those stinkin' sheep men to talk!'

'I know a man who has enough Mex blood in him to spout Mexican.' Ringold grinned. 'And he don't mind hurtin' folk if the price suits him.'

'Money's no object, hire him!' Petch snarled.

Petch gazed long and thoughtfully at his office wall after Ringold had left. Who the hell was this unknown Mexican who was carrying out a vendetta against him? And the bastard wasn't working on his own; there were at least two of them. That's why they had been able to do all the killing. But it was no good wondering who they were: catching them was all that mattered.

Gus Newton, the straw boss, had

interrupted him at breakfast and told him that a rider had come in with the news that the bank had been badly damaged in a botched raid and some of the gang had broken into the Long Branch, laid out Amiss and helped themselves to the contents of the safe.

Petch, being a one-time bank robber himself, knew exactly how the gang must have felt when their raid went wrong. Not wanting it to be a wasted night they had raided the nearest establishment they knew that would have a safe with cash in it, the saloon. He cold-smiled. Though their haul would be a damn sight lower than they had expected.

'Amiss said you had to be told it was the Mexican who took the cash, boss,' Newton continued. 'He must be one of the gang. The sheriff, after he'd had his two deputies shot down, ringed the bank with armed men but somehow the bastards slipped by them.'

Petch's smile faded. He sat in his chair for a minute or two in silence doing some hard and rapid thinking. Then, more to himself than at Newton, he said, 'There never was a gang of robbers. The bank was blown up by that Mex's pard to keep the sheriff, and everyone else in town, lookin' the wrong way while the big greaser took my cash.'

He tore the napkin from his neck and got to his feet, face working in anger, his appetite gone. 'Get my horse saddled up,' he snarled. 'And I want four hands to ride with me' The Mexican, whoever he was, was hitting him too close for comfort. His face hardened. He would see to it that every possible hideout in the territory was searched for signs of this mysterious Mexican. He would kick ass in the sheriff's office to make sure that Smithson earned the money he paid him. Then he'd pay a call on Elizabeta. Business would be quiet in the cat house this time of the day and she had a way of making him forget his troubles.

Ringold, drinking at the bar, was

thinking that this unknown greaser had Pearson real worried. Twice the Mexican had had a dig at him and he was getting the feeling that a part of Jackson Pearson's past life was catching up with him, and it wasn't a happy part.

Then, from out of the blue, Ringold got an uneasy thought that maybe Pearson's Mexican had a hand in the killing of his boys back there in Sonora. If the Mexican had found out that he worked for Pearson then it was bad medicine for him. The Mexican could turn his deadly attention on him and, Mex or not, he was an *hombre* who now knew the killing business. The roping in of the Mexican was now as much for his own peace of mind as Pearson's. Looking into the bar mirror he saw the man who could help him to find the Mexican push his way through the swing doors: Silvero, a mean-faced, part Mexican gunman, who had also ridden with old man Clanton's wild brood.

Ringold had seen the 'breed riding

into town late last night and guessed that the town-taming marshal of Tombstone had made it too hot for him and that he was looking for a quiet place to lie low for a spell where he didn't have to worry about the shotgun-carrying Earp, or his equally fast-shooting brothers, sneaking up on him.

Silvero, on seeing Ringegold at the bar, walked across and stood alongside him. Ringegold poured him out a shot of whiskey. He grinned, 'The Earps makin' it too hot for you in Tombstone, *amigo?*'

By the curses and dirty-mouthing Silvero heaped on the Earps and all their kin, Ringegold knew he had guessed right about the Mexican showing up unexpectedly in Gila Crossing.

'I've got a job for you, Silvero,' he said. 'It ain't sweat-raisin' or against the law.'

Silvero fixed a jaundiced-eyed side glance on Ringegold. 'I ain't been offered a job before that I ain't risked a hangin' doin' it, Rinegold. M'be I ain't hearin' right. All that dust I raised ass-kickin' it outa Tombstone must have kinda clogged up my ears.'

Rinegold grinned. 'You heard right, *amigo*: nothin' illegal and the pay's good. All you have to do to earn it is to throw a scare into a bunch of greasers — no offence meant — sheepherders, so that one of them will talk. Tell you where the tall Mex is, the man who's payin' us wants to have words with. Bein' your ma was Mexican you can question them in their own lingo. All me and the boys could get from the sonsuvbitches when we questioned them was that they didn't understand good old American talk. That's all you've got to do, Silvero; it'll be like money from home. Josh and Billy will be backin' you up.'

Gold-capped teeth glinted in the lamplight as Silvero gave a wolf's snarl of a grin. 'There'll be *señoritas* in this camp, no?'

'I reckon so,' replied Rinegold. 'You

can take what pleasures you want as long as you can get the information the boss man wants.'

* * *

'Here we are, boys,' Josh said, as he swung down from his saddle on the edge of the camp. 'Me and you, Billy, will take a stroll along that crick lookin' for holes, caves, whatever, where a man could lie low. That mysterious Mex ain't shacked up in the camp that's for sure, but he has to eat and he ain't doin' that in Gila Crossin' so he must be gettin' his chow from the sheepherders. You can disturb some of them havin' their siesta, Silvero, and start askin' your questions.'

Silvero had already picked out who he was going to question first: a young girl who was running into a patch of thick brush ahead of him. In her panicky rush her skirt snagged on a branch and he caught a glimpse of golden brown legs and thighs. He grinned at Josh and

Billy. Dismounting he walked across to the brush, saw-toothed spurs jangling and a fire burning hot in his groin.

Santos, sitting in his usual shaded place, spotted the three riders coming into the camp. He recognized the two gringos; one of them was the *hombre* whom he had almost killed, painfully. His eyes glinted savagely. They had come to question the sheepherders about the the whereabouts of the tall 'Mexican' again, and brought a Mexican along with them to do the asking. Petch was stepping up the hunt. His whole face took on a savage look when he saw the frightened *señorita* rush to hide in the brush and the Mexican dismount and head after her. Santos waited until the Mexican had gone from his sight then got to his feet. One quick glance towards the creek satisfied him that he couldn't be seen by either of the two gringos working their way along it. With his machete fisted he sped towards the brush, eyes red with the killing lust.

Marie lay in a tight huddled ball of fear, eyes closed. Her knuckles pressed into her mouth to prevent her from crying out her fears. Her father had told her that if the gringos showed up in the camp she had to hide for they were *mal hombres*, dogs who held no kindness towards Mexicans, and if the urge took them they would use her for their pleasures.

Silvero pushed his way through the undergrowth, cursing as a branch whipped back and scratched his face. 'Where are you, *señorita?*' he called out, trying to keep his voice as level as he could. He didn't want to scare her into making a run for it. He didn't want to have to chase the girl all over the camp in front of the mocking Billy and Josh. He stopped and listened, then smiled; he could hear the sound of stifled sobbing close by.

Marie, sensing imminent danger, opened her eyes. Though the man who was standing over her was a Mexican, the way he was looking at her chilled her blood. She let out a strangled cry of fear.

'Now you just lie there, *señorita*,' Silvero said. It won't take long then you can be on your way.' He began to unbuckle his belt grinning with lustful anticipation.

A terrified Marie sat numb-brained, unable to move as she realized her terrible fate. She closed her eyes and mouthed a silent prayer to the Holy *Madre* for her salvation.

A hand suddenly clamping over Silvero's mouth and yanking him back on to his heels, painfully and abruptly, ended his licentious thoughts. He had only a split-second of futile struggling to escape the vice-like grip of his attacker when he felt the nerve shrieking agony of a machete slicing across his throat then the warm flood of blood streaming down his chest. Santos held the body close to him until it had stopped jerking and twitching then let it fall to the ground.

'Go now, *señorita*,' he said softly. 'Go

to your home, this dog won't hurt you now.'

Marie risked opening her eyes and where her would-be ravisher had been standing was the fierce-looking old *hombre* who for the last few days had been staying in the camp. A man her father had said was a notorious *bandido* wanted by the *Federales* in Sonora for many killings and robberies. The sleeves of his shirt were dark with the blood of the bad *hombre* he had slain with the machete he still held in his hand. Her eyes widened in wonderment. The Holy *Madre* had sent a devil to save her from her terrible fate.

'*Vamoose*, girl!' Santos repeated. 'Those two gringos in the camp won't harm you.'

Marie smiled weakly, not trusting herself to voice her gratitude to her guardian devil. She gave a quick, but body-shuddering glance, at the butchered man before scrambling to her feet and running out into the open.

Santos wiped his machete clear of

148

blood on the shirt of the dead Silvero before hanging it back on to his belt. He drew out his pistol and cocked it. His killing fever was still running high. The Mexican would soon have company on his road to Hell. Stone-faced, he emerged from the brush.

It was Billy who saw the grim figure of their nemesis first. He had shouted across the creek to Josh that the ground on either side of the creek was levelling out and the only holes they would come across would be gopher holes.

'We'll head back to the camp, Josh,' he called. 'See how Silvero's doin'.' He grinned. 'I reckon he'll have humped that young *señorita* he was chasin' by now. If he's still enjoyin' himself we'll roust some of those greaser sheep men who're tryin' to fool us they're havin' their afternoon shuteye. Though this Mex comin' along the crick looks wide awake.' His voice rose a pitch. 'Why, I think it's the ugly-faced sonuvabitch who told me he couldn't savvy American.'

'M'be if you slip him a coupla silver dollars he'll find he can speak gringo,' Josh said. He grinned. 'Kindness works sometimes.'

Billy scowled, 'I'll bend my Colt barrel over his thick head if he plays dumb again.' Then he gave out with a yell of alarm. 'The bastard's fistin' a gun!' And he clawed for his own pistol.

Without pausing in his stride Santos brought up his gun and pulled off a shot. The shell punched a crimson-ringed hole in the centre of Billy's brow, blowing away the back of his head as it exited before Billy's pistol had cleared the holster. A truly dead man, he pitched headfirst into the creek.

Santos swung his pistol on to Josh. The quick killing of Billy had unnerved him somewhat, slowing his action in yanking out his gun. The shot that hit him between the shoulders and sent him spreadeagled on to the ground, as dead as Billy, had been discharged from a rifle.

Santos looked across the creek to the high ground and saw Raynor up on his horse silhouetted on the ridge. He heard faintly a call of, 'I thought you could need a hand, *amigo*, takin' on two fearsome gringo *pistoleros*!'

Santos snarled and spat on the ground. Back shooters more likely, he thought.

Raynor let his horse pick its own way down from the ridge and splash across the creek to join Santos. His face hardened as he saw the dark stains on his *compadre*'s shirt. He swung up his rifle. 'Any more of the bastards in the camp, José?' he asked.

Santos smiled. 'Not alive, *amigo*,' he replied 'This time Petch sent a Mexican with those gringos. I cut the dog's throat back there in the brush. He was about to deflower a young *señorita*.'

Raynor sat thinking in his saddle for a minute or two. 'Petch is hottin' up the search for that 'Mexican',' he said, 'by sendin' a Mexican to do the questionin'. If you hadn't been around, that fella whose throat you slit, would have forced that *señorita*, or someone else in the camp, until they let slip that the *bandido*, José Santos, had showed up in their camp. Petch, on hearing that news will soon figure out who the tall Mexican is and will no longer be frustrated wonderin' who the hell's been hittin' him. And we'll have lost our edge.' Raynor favoured his partner with a flint-eyed look. 'It's time we upped the stakes, bring things to a head, like doin' some burnin' out along Main Street. And finish off what we came here to do.'

* * *

Ringold drew up his mount and took in the big house set back from the creek. He was out doing a lone scout to find the whereabouts of the Mexican. He had heard that its owner was an Eastern dude who had once owned the Long Branch saloon and the cat house before he came to Gila Crossing. Then the Easterner had been bushwhacked by parties unknown and left to get about with the aid of two sticks. Pearson now owned both establishments. Ringold slow-smiled. The rancher sure had a tough, but efficient way of doing business.

He could see several barns at the rear of the house where a man could lie low for a spell if the owner of the property was a cripple and had no hired hands doing his chores. For his own sake, his search for the Mexican had to be thorough, even if it meant knocking on the front door of a man who would give him short shrift if he so much as suspected that he worked for Pearson, and asking him if he had seen a Mexican ride across his land.

Ringold soon found out how much of a risk he was taking. He had twenty feet or so to make it to the house when he saw movement at the far end of the front porch, then the ominous glint of the long barrel of a shotgun poking across the porch rail. Ringold held his breath and, with the minimum of hand movement, brought his horse to a halt.

'You turn your horse around, mister, and head back for the trail; you're ridin' on private land!' a voice called out.

Ringegold caught a glimpse of a huddled figure in a chair. The dude may be a cripple but not crippled enough not to be able to pull the trigger of a shotgun.. He raised both hands slowly. 'I ain't lookin' for trouble, mister,' he said. 'I only wanted to ask you if I'm on the right trail to Gila Crossin',' he lied.

'Follow the creek eastwards,' Lassiter snapped back. 'Or you'll be riding along a trail that's got no way back!'

Ringegold reckoned he knew when a man was bluffing; he had done some bluffing himself when it was required, but right now he was listening to a man who meant what he said. It was eat-crow-time if he didn't want to be blown out of his saddle. He lowered his hands and tugged his horse's head round and rode back down to the main trail.

Lassiter lowered the shotgun and laid it upright in the corner of the porch, ready to be picked up again if needed. He had no doubt that the rider was one of Petch's gunmen searching for John Raynor. He had a good feeling, the first since his bushwacking, that he was at last fighting back against the son-of-a-bitch, Petch.

★   ★   ★

Ringold dismounted outside the Long Branch feeling that he was entitled to a drink after his long, but fruitless search for the Mexican. He had just hitched his horse to the rail when Slattery, one of his original cattle-lifting gang, burst out of the saloon.

'Josh, Billy and the 'breed came into town roped across the backs of their horses as dead as any man can be!' he called out. 'The 'breed had his throat sliced open, the other two were shot! What sort of man is this Mex, Ringold? He's chalked up six kills already. The talk in the saloon is that he's only one of a bunch of Mex *bandidos* who are raidin' from across the border. Me and Benteen are thinkin' about riding back to Tombstone and join up with Clanton and his boys again. At least you can see the Earps movin' around and get holed-up someplace. That Mex sneaks around like a full blood Injun.'

Ringold didn't want to upset Slattery more than he was already by telling him that the Mex's total of kills could be six more if he counted the boys who had been gunned down in Sonora. He was now getting more than a gut feeling that the Mexican had been one of the unknown guns firing at them through the prairie fire. Though his immediate worry was to stop Slattery and Benteen quitting on him, or he would have no gang at all.

'There's no need to fret, Slattery,' he replied confidently. 'All right this Mex has shot some of the fellas who are tryin' to track him down, but he ain't killed anyone here in town, has he? He ain't about to jump outa a side alley across the way there and cut loose at us. As you say he does his killin' Injun style. I reckon when he figures he has the edge. But I'll tell you this, Slattery, the next time we go out there'll be a big bunch of us, enough guns to take on a whole bunch of Mex *bandidos*. I'll tell Pearson that when I see him.' He glanced along at the cat house. 'Though it'll not be tonight, his horse ain't hitched up outside the cat house. He'll be back at the the XL. Let's go into the saloon and join Benteen.' He grinned. 'Then later pass an hour or so with those fine ladies next door. Which is a damn sight more pleasurable pastime than playin' cards with the Clanton boys in their hog pen of a bunkhouse.'

'Yeah I guess so,' replied Slattery as he followed Ringold into the saloon. He couldn't deny that he and Benteen had been well paid for their cattle-lifting trips into Sonora. Allowing them to spend like high rolling gents in the saloon and the cat house. Though that did not prevent him from worrying about the Mexican and at the ease in which he was gunning down some of the men he'd liquored up with.

Ringegold's insides were also acting up. Pearson's mysterious Mexican enemy was getting under his skin. Ringegold was a professional gun, not a face-to-face shoot-out killer, unless he judged that he would be left standing after the shooting. What was troubling him was that he couldn't see this Mexican *pistolero* allowing a gringo to sneak up on him. Men who had met up with him ended up dead.

As he ordered drinks for the three of them, still smiling his snake-oil pedlar's grin, he promised himself that if Pearson didn't show up in town tomorrow he would ride out to the XL and have words with Pearson in his den. And to hell with the son-of-a-bitch not wanting to rub shoulders in public with a man who had warrants posted on him. Pearson's public image ran second to Johnny Rinegold's need to stay alive.

Ex-Sheriff Smithson was also in the saloon, sitting alone at a table getting himslf drunk, too down in spirits to partake of further sins of the flesh such as having a session with the blood-stirring blonde in the sporting house.

Early on in the day, Petch had stormed into his office looking mad enough to shoot him for not roping in the deadly shooting Mexican.

'Since that Mex shot down my two deputies, Mr Pearson,' he said. 'No man in town will take a deputy's badge. And I can't hunt him down on my own!' he added defensively.

Petch gave him the evil eye. 'Get out and earn your pay, you old soak! Bring the state marshals in!' He turned and strode out of the office, banging the door behind him with such force that it almost jumped off its hinges.

Scowling, Sheriff Smithson sat at his desk thinking over things for about an hour. Finally he came to a decision.

Being called an old soak, even though it was true, was the last shaming he would take from Mr 'All Mighty' Pearson. He unclipped his badge from his vest and laid it down on the table and got to his feet. Not bothering to lock up the office, he made his way across the street to the Long Branch, just in time to see the Mexican's latest handiwork with his guns coming into town, laid across the backs of their horses; now no business of his, and thought that quitting the sheriff's job was one of the wisest decisions he had ever made in his life.

If Pearson wanted the Mex so badly he should ride out with the four boys he had brought with him and seek him out. And let them risk coming back into town slung across their horses' asses. Smithson gave a drunk's slack-faced smile. When Pearson got to hear of the Mex's latest kills he would have his whole crew riding as shotgun over him. With an unsteady hand he poured himself out another full glass of liquid comfort.

14

Raynor and Santos came into Gila Crossing after the lamps in the Long Branch and the cat house had been lit and all the other buildings fronting Main Street were in darkness. Their horses were tethered in a stand of timber on the outskirts of the town and they strode along the boardwalk, mingling with the townsfolk as though they were a couple of ranch hands out for a night's drinking. Raynor was wearing his normal range gear, no longer the tall Mexican.

Before coming into town he had checked with Lassiter on the whereabouts of Petch. He knew that when Petch was in town he spent a lot of his time in the cat house. His presence there would scotch his plan of robbing the house's safe. He wasn't ready yet to have a face-to-face shoot-out with Petch.

'No, Petch isn't in town,' Lassiter had said. 'Him and his four men crossed the creek four hours ago making for his ranch.'

'Has any other rider, one in a helluva hurry, come by this way within the last coupla hours or so, headin' for the XL?' Raynor asked.

'No,' replied Lassiter. 'Just Petch and his ranch hands have forded the creek. Why do you ask?'

Raynor then told Lassiter about Santos's killings at the sheepherders' camp.

'God Almighty!' gasped Lassiter, half rising out of his chair. 'Between you, you've put paid to six of Petch's bully boys!'

Raynor's lips twitched in a ghost of a smile. 'Twelve, Mr Lassiter. We downed six cattle-lifters in Sonora on the way here. Though we didn't know it at the time that the bastards were stealin' cattle for Petch. But we had good reason to send them on their way to Hell. Now it's about time me and

Santos got ourselves ready to empty the whorehouses's strong box then put a torch to it and the saloon before some righteous-minded citizen takes it in his head to ride out to the XL to let Petch know about the latest shootin' down of his men, and have him fire-ballin' in with his crew and rousin' up the whole town. The townsfolk on the street would upset my and Santos's plans.' He gave Lassiter a goodbye nod and rode out.

Lassiter watched him go, still trying to take in the big Texan's matter-of-fact account of his and his partner's killings. Santos, he reckoned, in his *bandido* days must have caused the Mexican lawmen one hell of a headache. And Raynor had proved that he was no mean player in the killing stakes. And here the pair were, about to give Petch one last headache before finally settling up their score with him. Then he wondered if he could see the flames of the burning saloon and cat house from his usual seat on the porch.

The tapping on the rear door of his store came as Farrow was doing his accounts. He knew who it would be, though what the tall Texan wanted from him this time had him puzzled. One thing he was sure of as he unlocked the door was that Petch was about to have another load of trouble heaped on him. Trouble, he figured, that would be worth missing sleep again to watch. Farrow quickly shut and locked the door behind his nocturnal visitors as soon as they had stepped into the store. He turned and looked up at Raynor.

'What can I do for you this time, Mr Raynor?' he asked, eager to get them off his premises and back on to the street. Death hung over them like an invisible shroud.

'A store suit, Mr Farrow,' Raynor said. 'The last time we were here I noticed you had some suits hangin' on a rail.'

'A suit!' repeated Farrow, slack-jawed with surprise.

'Yeah, that's right,' replied Raynor. 'And my *amigo*, would like a can of coal oil.'

A suit and coal oil! Farrow was somewhat confused. Coal oil meant a burning out so the hardnosed pair were stepping up their war against Petch. Though how the suit fitted in with the Texan's fight against Petch had him foxed. And he hadn't the guts to ask him why he needed the suit. Then Raynor answered his unspoken question.

'I'm goin' to pay a visit to the whorehouse, Mr Farrow,' Raynor said. 'Not to indulge in the pleasures that can be bought there, but to rob the safe. Saturdays and today are busy times for the place and what cash the girls have brought in will be in the safe until the bank opens in the mornin'. I need to stroll in the place dressed like a Texas cattle buyer, not like some asshole of a drifter. I've got to win the confidence of the madam — the safe's in her room.' He favoured Farrow with a bared-toothed grin. 'While I'm in there Señor Santos will be burnin' down the saloon. Some general or other once said that if you can confuse your enemy you're halfway to winnin' the battle. Before this night is over Petch is goin' to be one confused *hombre*, along with most of the town.'

Farrow's blood chilled. He was trying to live up to his late grandpappy's true grit days by making a stand against Petch. But he knew he lacked the fighting spirit to burn down buildings and rob safes as though they were everyday chores.

'I've a suit that oughta fit you, Mr Raynor,' he said. 'And a dress shirt to go with it. And there's some cans of coal oil in the back storeroom.' Farrow wasn't about to tell the bone-faced Texan that the suit was Henry Logan's laying out gear; his widow was due to pick it up in the morning. He didn't know if badasses like Raynor and his Mex pard were superstitious characters, believing in omens like not wearing a dead man's suit, as he didn't want to deter them from putting the torch to Petch's money-making establishments in town. While he was sitting at his window waiting for the joyous moment when he saw the first of the flames lighting up Main Street, he would alter the jacket of one of the other suits he had left to fit the broad shoulders of the late Henry Logan.

He forced out a weak grin. 'There's no charge for either item.'

Before Raynor and Santos parted outside the rear of the store to go their own grim ways, Raynor to walk along Main Street to the whorehouse, Santos to sneak along the empty back lots, the tin of coal oil hidden under his *serape*, to do his fire-raising, Raynor asked Santos if the sheepherders had broken up their camp.

'They'll not be safe there after the killings,' Raynor said.

'*Sí, amigo,*' replied Santos. 'By now their families, with the sheep, will have a new camp in a blind canyon several miles south, where there is water and grass for the herds. I gave the *jefe* the guns and reloads we took off the gringos we killed.'

'*Bueno*,' said Raynor. 'I didn't want them dragged into our war, but they're sure deep in it now. It's only right for us to look out for them. See to it that Petch and his men do them no harm.'

'Never fear, Juan,' Santos said. 'Those *hombres* are well armed and will fight to protect their families and herds.' He gave one of his fearsome *bandido* grins. 'Some of those *pacificos* fought as *Juaristas* against the French and their emperor who once ruled Mexico. Petch can be as loco as he wants, but his men aren't mad. They're only fighting because they're on his payroll. When the *hombres* start shooting them out of their saddles some of them will wish they had stayed tendin' the cows.'

'Yeah,' replied Raynor. 'Those ranch hands will reckon that a dollar and three squares a day ain't much recompense for riskin' havin' lumps of lead shot into their hides. OK, we've done all we're beholden to do for those sheepherders, let's go and wake up this dog-dirt burg.'

The weekend trade was beginning to pick up in the cat house and Madame Elizabeta just inside the porch entrance smiled at the regulars who came through the door. Standing slightly behind her was a hard-eyed bull of a man, the estabishment's bouncer. A frowning glance from Madame Elizabeta and some too rowdy drunk client would find himself lying on his ass in the middle of Main Street. Elizabeta ran a high-class house, and would have no roughnecks damaging her reputation.

Elizabeta's fixed-eyed welcoming smile sharpened into one of curious interest as her latest client came into the porch. He was a tall man, dressed in a store suit though he wore a wide-brimmed plains hat and spurred boots. She had never seen him in the cat house before.

His hard-boned face was in keeping with the belted pistol bulging out the tails of his tight fitting coat. A sure judge of men, naked or fully dressed, Elizabeta came quickly to the conclusion that the stranger was no drummer. He had the all-seeing stare and stance of the men she had seen portrayed in a dime magazine some Eastern salesman had left in one of the rooms, the tall riding men from the Missourian backwoods, notorious bank and train robbers. But he couldn't be a bank robber, she thought. What the hell would a bank robber be doing in Gila Crossing when there was only half a bank left standing? She fingered him as a state marshal. Still smiling and with a hip-swaying walk she stepped across the room to greet him.

Raynor halted and waited for the well-rounded woman to come up to him. With her long raven-black hair held back from her olive-skinned face by two silver combs he opined she was Petch's bed companion and the madam of the house. And even he knew that the gown she had on and the jewellery she was wearing must have set Petch back a small fortune. A part of his and Santos's fortune he thought wryly. He politely removed his hat and smiled down at her.

'Ma'am,' he said. 'A man would have to ride a long ways to find a finer-lookin' cat house.' Then realizing the urgency to put the madam at her ease he laid on the charm, broadening his smile. 'And that goes for the owner as well.'

Elizabeta blushed, for the first time in over forty years. And wondering, professionally, how the tall stranger would perform between the sheets. Not that she took clients to her room since she had been Pearson's woman, but it was something to fantasize about. Then she got a grip on her wayward thoughts. Her smile froze slightly. Was the big son-of-a-bitch joshing her? Was he trying to wheedle round her with his mealy-mouthed words so he could have a night's free humping, she thought

171

angrily? Elizabeta looked him directly in the eye but could see no hidden mockery or shiftiness in the unblinking gaze. Her anger died away.

'I'm Elizabeta, Mr . . . er,' she said. 'I run this house, but I'm not the owner.'

Then, in spite of controlling her feelings, she still felt attracted by the big man, she broke the golden rule of the great plains hospitality by asking a stranger what business had brought him to Gila Crossing.

She was close enough to Raynor for him to smell her perfume and feel the heat of her bared shoulders, which gave him the burning urge to bounce her in one of the rooms upstairs, if she was still a working girl. But he was here for business, not to cool his blood. It wouldn't be long before Santos set fire to the saloon and he had to play his part.

'Will Bodine,' he said. 'A cattle buyer. I've heard there's a big cattle spread not far from Gila Crossin'. I'm hopin' to do business with the owner.'

If you're a cattle buyer, Mr Bodine, Elizabeta thought, then I'm running a nunnery here. You're a hard-nosed state lawman, that's who. Smiling, she reached out a hand and took Raynor's in a firm, friendly handshake. 'Welcome to Gila Crossing, Mr Bodine, cattle buyer.' She put her arm through his. 'Let's go and meet some of my girls.' and she walked him into the lounge, where most of the sofas and easy chairs were occupied by the well-heeled store-suited citizens of the town being served drinks by girls showing more flesh than he had seen any female showing for a long time.

Now came the hard part of their plan. In fact the more he thought about their plan to rob the cat house safe the more crazy it became. If he did get in the room where the safe was how the hell was he going to open it. The woman on his arm had access to the keys. He couldn't stick his pistol in her ribs and force her upstairs and demand that she opened the safe. The big ape in the doorway wasn't standing there as an ornament. Any sign of trouble and he would haul out the hideaway gun he wore. Some of the gents who were working up a healthy sweat larking with the girls would be sporting pistols and, before he could spit, he would be the main target in a one-sided gun fight. And he had only one pistol, six shells, with no time to reload, to defend himself with. His other pistol and his normal clothes were in a bundle strapped on his horse. They should have been satisfied with just robbing and burning down the saloon, he thought dourly.

It was Elizabeta who solved his dilemma, and proving to Raynor that the good fortune he and Santos had enjoyed since coming to Gila Crossing was still riding with them.

'Do you want a drink, Mr Bodine?' she asked.

Keen to get upstairs, that much closer to the safe, Raynor shook his head. 'If I wanted a drink I would have gone into the saloon.' He gave Elizabeta a leer of a grin. 'And besides, seein' all those purty young females kinda puts a man off wastin' his time drinkin'.'

Elizabeta grinned back at him. Horn dogs came in all shapes and sizes, she thought. 'Mr Bodine,' she said, 'we are here to please our clients. And there's a girl upstairs who is an expert in quenching any man's thirst. I'll take you to her room.'

And again she put her arm through Raynor's and led him to the stairs, Raynor praying that Santos wasn't about to start his fire in the saloon. That would set everyone in the cat house haring out on to the street for a looksee, including the hot-blooded madam clinging to him, his only lead to getting the safe open.

At the head of the stairs ran a long, thick carpeted corridor and Raynor saw that the first door on the right showed a brass plate with 'Private' engraved on it.

'Is that your room, ma'am?' Raynor asked nodding to the door.

'My room and the office,' Elizabeta replied. She grinned. 'But it's Red's room you want.' Then she gave out with an alarmed cry of, 'What the hell! — ' as Mr Bodine grabbed her tight around the waist, his other hand clamping over her mouth, choking off her cries. She felt herself being bodily lifted and dragged back to her room.

Raynor had no time to waste seeing if the door was locked he heaved himself at it and the door burst in. He pulled the wildly struggling, muffled-voice shouting Elizabeta in with him and back-heeled the door shut.

Elizabeta wouldn't have minded a session with Mr Bodine, but to have him take her, unasked, like some savage Indian, quickly extinguished the warm feelings she had felt toward him. Then Mr Bodine's arm released its vice-like grip and his hand now held a pistol pressed to her head and Elizabeta's fears were not that she was expecting to be raped, but for her life. An uncontrollable fear clawed sickeningly at her throat. Then she heard Mr Bodine say, 'I'm going to take my hand from your mouth, ma'am, but if you so much as squeak I'll lay this pistol hard against your purty head, *comprende*?'

Elizabeta, especially when she was a lot younger, and was working in the rough border saloons and bordellos, had been used to all manner of looks from her clients, but she had never experienced such a savage mask of a look before. She just knew that she was going to be brutally used then shot. She sobbed helplessly. And she had thought that Mr Bodine was an upright lawman. With tear-filled eyes she nodded.

Raynor warily took his hand from her mouth. He breathed a silent sigh of relief. He seemed to have scared her enough for her not to call his bluff and yell her head off. He was a hard man, had gunned down men who had stood between him and an open safe, but he he knew he would chicken out of cold cocking a fine-looking female.

'Good,' he growled. 'Now just open that safe and I'll take what cash there's in there and be on my way. And apologize for any upset I've caused you.'

Elizabeta blinked back her tears and gazed at Raynor with surprise. 'Rob the safe? I thought that you were going to use me for free like some drunken ranch hand!'

Raynor's face reddened. 'Do I look like a horn dog rapist?' he spluttered.

'I thought that you were a state marshal,' Elizabeta replied angrily, regaining some of her nerve. She gave him a look of contempt. 'I didn't figure you as a penny-ante sneak thief only having the balls to rob a cat-house safe! Do you roll drunks in side alleys as well?' Elizabeta was more angry with herself than at Raynor for being so wrong in judging him as a lawman.

Raynor roped in his anger. The *señora* was entitled to say what she thought about him after the fright he had given her. But, almost snarling, he said, 'I don't roll drunks! That money in the safe, and a whole heap more, belongs to me and my pard. Stolen from us by your boss, Mr Pearson. Though when we rode together as a gang of bank robbers in Texas he went by the name of Jake Petch!'

Pearson ... Petch, the man who regularly shared her bed, a bank robber? Elizabeta gasped in disbelief. Though confused by Raynor's statement, she was still angry enough to bold-eye him and say, 'Do you want my rings and necklaces, Mr Bodine? Mr Pearson bought them for me. By what you've just told me they rightly belong to you and your partner!'

'Quit needlin' me, ma'am,' Raynor replied still gravel-voiced. 'And get that safe open, or so help me, I'll forget my gentlemanly manners and bounce my Colt on your head!'

Elizabeta had the savvy to realize she had prodded Mr Bodine as far as she dared. If he had told her right about Pearson being a former bank robber who had wronged him in some deal or other, she'd be damned if she was going to get her head cracked open protecting the money in the safe. The key was in a heavy ashtray on the table by the bedhead and she walked across and picked it up, came back and handed it to Raynor.

'It's your money, so you say, so take it out of the safe yourself,' she said in a final act of defiance.

A suspicious-eyed Raynor took it off her then made her stand in a corner of the room, well away from the door, and where he could see her while he opened the safe. By the way the madam had just mouthed off at him she seemed to have lost her fear of him. It could come to laying her out with his pistol before the money was in his pockets. He couldn't tell Santos that a female had prevented him from opening the safe. Then he began to worry that it was time Santos had started his fire. He had heard no shots so he reckoned that the old *bandido* hadn't run into any trouble, but the delay was worrying him.

Santos had run into a slight snag that had delayed him for several minutes from setting fire to the saloon. He'd had to wait in the deeper darkness between some outbuildings while two men were stacking crates at the rear of the saloon. By the light streaming out of the open door he could see that one of them had a bandage wrapped around his head. He would be the manager, the man Juan had cold cocked. If the gringo sons-of-bitches didn't get him and his hired hand inside soon he would need another bandage around his head, Santos muttered. And he began to get impatient. Juan would be wondering why he wasn't getting his diversionary fire. His *amigo* was in danger every minute he was in the whorehouse.

He was all set to light-foot it across to the two men and down them both with his pistol silently. It was too dark to risk slashing their throats with his machete, expert though he was in that death-dealing skill. A yell from one of them and the alarm would be raised and he could be of no help to Juan.

Santos had to put up with a few more minutes of cursing before the men finished their chore and walked back inside the saloon. Then he was on the move, pistol held ready, the coal oil sloshing in the can. Stopping just outside the doorway he didn't waste any more time. He quickly unscrewed the cap off the can and splashed some of its contents along the passageway as far as he could, and over the feet of the loud cursing barkeep who was coming back along the passage.

Santos was on to him wielding his pistol before the man got over his shock and raised the alarm. Holding the unconscious man across his shoulder, he dragged him out into the open and dropped him to the ground. He then thumbed a match into flame and tossed it through the doorway.

The oil ignited with a roar, and the

unexpected back blow of the flames shooting out into the yard singed Santos's eyebrows and *serape* causing him to stagger back doing some more cursing.

A wall of flame gushed through the door leading into the bar and created immediate panic. Shouting and yelling, the customers and saloon girls over-turned tables and chairs as they made a mad dash for the street. The saloon manager watched with fascinated horror the flames licking around the edge of his bar. He could see that it was way past forming a chain of water-filled pails, the flames had too great a hold. Grabbing hold of the till he followed the last of his customers out of the saloon.

Out in the centre of Main Street, an unsteady-legged, smirking, ex-Sheriff Smithson watched the flames shooting through the windows and eaves of the saloon. He knew who had started the inferno. The tall Mexican was having another dig at the 'Big *hombre*', Mr

Pearson. He wished the unknown greaser all the luck in the world in his campaign against him.

Raynor had the cash from the safe in his pocket, now he was faced with another hard part of the plan to hit the saloon and the cat house together: what to do with the *señora*. If he just left her in the room, as soon as he closed the door behind him, she would raise the roof and he would have to gun his way out of the building. And he hadn't the time to bind and gag her. He would have to be as hard as his partner would be if he was standing in his place.

Elizabeta bit at her lower lip nervously. She knew the big man was deciding her fate. Bank robbers were hard, unkindly men; men facing a hanging if caught by the law. Her death and injury would be of little consequence to Mr Bodine.

A loud knocking at her door and shouts of, 'The saloon's on fire, *señora*, we're goin' down into the street to have a closer look!' had them both swinging round to face the door. Then came the clatter of shoes as the girls ran down the stairs.

Elizabeta saw the slight easing of the tension in Mr Bodine's face and surprising herself by her boldness she said, 'Your partner's set fire to the saloon, hasn't he, Mr Bodine?'

'That he has, *señora*,' replied Raynor. 'And he's goin' to put the torch to this place as well.'

'*Madre de Dios*!' breathed a shock-faced Elizabeta. 'You must have a big hate for Mr Pearson. What did he do to you both, try to kill you?'

'The sonuvabitch thought he had,' Raynor told her, his voice as hard-toned as his face.

It took Elizabeta a few minutes for that matter-of-fact statement to sink in, and know that it didn't improve her likelihood of walking out of the room unharmed. Though she had already accepted that her well-being was running along a thin line, a flaming anger took over her. She glared at Raynor.

'What have my girls got to do with your vendetta against Pearson!' she cried, wild-eyed. 'They're out on the street now and if this place goes up in flames they'll be risking their lives trying to get to their rooms to rescue what clothes they've got and the few extra dollars clients have tipped them. Burning down this place won't hurt Pearson, he's rich enough to build another one, but it will take my girls a long time to make up what they could lose, and Pearson won't help them out!' She gave Raynor a final cutting look before saying, 'You may not roll drunks, Mr Bodine, but you'll rob hard-working cat-house girls!' Elizabeta was satisfied she had said her piece, the hard-faced bastard could do no more harm to her than he had already decided to do.

Raynor was somewhat taken aback by the *señora*'s sudden outburst of defiance. It seemed that he hadn't scared her as much as he thought he had. And what she had said struck home. John Raynor, bank robber, *desperado*, now a robber of whores' hard-earned takings. A decision had to be taken about the *señora*, quickly. Santos would be close by somewhere, waiting with his can of coal oil and a great hate to set fire to Petch's property, wondering why it was taking so long for his *amigo* to rob an office safe.

'Señora,' he said, 'I'll make a deal with you. You stay quiet until I'm clear of the buildin' and I'll stop my pard from destroyin' it.' He gimlet-eyed Elizabeta. 'Is it a deal? You know the alternative.'

'It's a deal, Mr Bodine,' replied a not-so-bold-feeling Elizabeta, who was not expecting a deal of any sort from Mr Bodine. 'You have my word on it.'

'That's good enough for me, *señora*,' Raynor said. Whether Santos would think likewise he would soon find out, but he had to sweet talk the hot-blooded Santos to accept it. A deal was a deal and his word was as good as a whorehouse madam's.

In spite of Mr Bodine having almost scared her to death, Elizabeta, for some unexplained reason, called out, 'You take care, Mr Bodine,' as he left the room. Then she flopped down on her bed as weak and trembling as if she'd had a heavy session with the whole crew of some ranch or other.

'OK, *amigo?*' Raynor heard, as he stepped into the open. He had come down the back stairs, seeing no one, and hearing no hysterical female screams behind him that the safe had been robbed. He thin-smiled. In another place, another time, he would have enjoyed humping the high-spirited *señora*.

'Everything's fine, Santos,' he replied. 'I've got the contents of the safe.' The flames of the burning saloon lit up the back lots, and wind-driven sparks were starting small brush fires on the open ground that led down to Gila Creek. Raynor grinned. 'When you start a fire, *compadre*, you sure as hell start one. But we ain't burnin' down the cat house. I'll tell you why later. Let's get the horses before any *hombres* come by this way and start askin' what you're holdin' in your hand, backin' their questions with a pointed gun.' Without giving Santos any time to speak he turned and ran towards where they had tethered their horses.

Raynor heard the thud of the can hitting the ground then the sound of Santos cursing as he caught up with him. He gave a relieved smile; he hadn't expected his partner to give in so easily. The *señora* would be finding out that a bank-robber's word could be relied on.

Once clear of the town, Raynor told Santos of the deal he had made with the whorehouse madam. 'She kinda caught me on the raw, *amigo*,' he said. 'Accusin' me of robbin' her hard-workin' girls.' He grinned across at Santos. 'And you oughta know how hard those fallen doves work. And it's not that we ain't hurt Petch real bad back there in town, Santos. We've made him lose face again, in front of folk he wants to impress as bein' king pin in the territory.'

Santos gave a grunt which Raynor took as an acceptance of the way he had played things in the cat house.

'But we've shown our hands, *compadre*,' Raynor continued. 'Petch will soon know that he didn't finish us off at Sawmill Creek. He'll be bound to seek us out at the sheepherders' camp, with some force, to make sure he kills us dead this time. Those *hombres* will need every gun they can muster. You ride there, *amigo*, and get them organized. I'll join you once I've let Lassiter know that things went our way in town.' He grinned. 'And don't forget to tell the *hombres* that the lone gringo comin' is an *amigo*.'

Raynor got another assenting grunt from his partner as he swung away from him to ride to the lonely house at the creek crossing.

It was too dark for Raynor to see Lassiter sitting on his front porch, but as he drew up his horse he picked out the red glowing tip of his cigar and caught a smell of its strong tangy smoke.

'We've pulled it off, Mr Lassiter!' he said. 'Petch's saloon is still burnin' and we've got the cash he had stashed away in the whorehouse's safe. Though the *señora* boss lady prevailed on me not to burn the place down. She told me I was makin' war on innocent girls.'

'The *señora*,' Lassiter said, 'is a persuasive female. She's well liked by her girls, looks after them. She's also well liked by Mr 'Pearson', if you follow my drift, Mr Raynor.'

'I told her some home truths about Mr Pearson,' Raynor said. 'So she might not be so friendly towards him now. It's just as well because the sonuvabitch's days are numbered.'

'Are you stepping down and coming in for a drink, coffee, whiskey, Mr Raynor?' Lassiter asked.

'I'd like nothin' better, Mr Lassiter,' replied Raynor. 'But I haven't got the time; Santos is expectin' me at the sheepherders' camp. Twice Petch has sent out men to the camp to look for the Mexican who's causin' him a whole heap of trouble and when he hears of his latest misfortunes he'll pay that camp another visit, backed up by most of his crew. The sheepherders and their families, along with their sheep, are forted up in a box canyon, armed up and ready to make a fight of it when Petch shows up. With me and Santos backin' them up they should do more than hold their own.' Raynor's voice and face hardened. 'Bully boys or not, we'll break the bastards, Mr Lassiter, then Petch will be on his own. Me and Santos will pay him a call and get our blood payment from him. Not forgettin' to pick up whatever he's holdin' in the safe.'

Raynor kneed his mount into a gentle canter and, before he was swallowed up in the dark, Lassiter heard a faint 'Buenos noches', drifting back on the night air.

Lassiter raised his hand in a farewell

gesture in the direction of the sound of the fading hoofs. He could not ever remember being concerned about anyone but himself, but he was worrying about Mr Raynor, a man of his own stamp. The odds were stacking up against him and his partner. Mexican sheepherders were not reckoned to be wild blood men, generally raising hell like a bunch of hard-assed ranch hands regularly did on pay days. But the pair were driven by their stubborn pride to settle a debt that could only be wiped out by blood, Petch's blood, and odds weren't calculated in those kind of settlements. He wished them both all the luck they would need and settled down in his chair, pulling the blanket closer about him, to catch the first sight of Petch, and the men riding with him, as they forded the creek. Then he would see just how high the odds were against Raynor and Santos. And curse because he couldn't be at their side to help them out.

15

Rinegold had watched the fiery destruction of the saloon and was now standing gazing at its charred, still smoking ruins. He had to admit that Pearson's mysterious Mexican was a real hell raiser. And the son-of-a-bitch wasn't alone. According to the cathouse madam it was an Anglo who had robbed her safe. That confirmed his belief that it was the Mexican who had ambushed them in Sonora, the other rifle firing at him and his boys must have been held by the American safe robber.

Rinegold was also sure that their disagreement with Pearson was coming to a final bloody conclusion. As slick as they had been so far in their deadly actions against the rancher, the killings, the safe robberies and now the burning down of the saloon, they'd be on the losing side when Pearson, on hearing of his fine saloon being gutted, set up a big hunt for them. And he would ride with him to make sure that the two hard men were gunned down. He didn't want the pair to hound him down for the killing of the three sheepherders in Sonora.

'I was on a winnin' streak,' Benteen moaned, he and Slattery were standing alongside Ringold. 'When the fire burst through into the bar I made a grab for the pot but before I could get my hands on all that foldin' money the table was overturned and I was knocked on my ass by the drinkers at the bar harin' it for the street.'

'Me and Slattery had our pleasures cut short in the cat house,' Ringold said. 'We were halfway through our session when the fire started. All the girls ran out to the street to get a closer look at the blaze leavin' us lyin' there with our pants off in one helluva sweat. Ain't that so, Slattery?'

Slattery didn't answer him. Fish-eying

Rinegold, he said, 'You were right about that Mex not gunnin' us down from some alley, Rinegold. The sonuvabitch intended roasting us all to death.'

'What do we do now, Rinegold?' Benteen asked. 'I ain't stoppin' in a town that's got no saloon.'

Rinegold felt it was time he showed that he was the man who gave out the orders. 'We grab ourselves a few hours' sleep; we'll have a busy day ahead of us.' He grinned at the surprised-looking Slattery and Benteen. 'I told you, Slattery, that we wouldn't go huntin' that Mex unless there's a whole bunch of us. When Pearson hears about his fine saloon bein' burnt down you can bet your bottom dollar that he'll come ass-kickin' into town with every hand he's got, includin' his Chinese cook, as soon as it's light enough to see that the Mex and his gringo partner ain't hidin' behind some rock with long guns in their hands somewhere along the trail.'

'If he's comin' in with a small army,' Benteen said, 'he don't need our three guns; we can ride back to Tombstone and some saloons.'

Ringegold's voice steeled over. 'We're joinin' in the hunt for the Mexican and whoever's ridin' with him, Benteen. They were the bastards who started the fire that stampeded the herd we were drivin' north and gunned down Frank and Slim and the rest of the boys. I reckon it's beholden on us to make them pay for gunnin' down our pards. OK?'

'That puts a different slant on things, Ringegold,' Benteen said. 'I'm willin' to ride with you.'

'Me and Frank were close buddies,' Slattery said. 'It'll give me great pleasure to gut shoot that Mex. Count me in, Ringegold.'

Ringegold gave an inner satisfied grin. He still had a gang. Maybe a small one, but big enough for him to give out orders.

'OK, boys,' he ordered. Let's get a coupla hours of sleep then be already mounted up when Pearson and his crew ride in.'

16

Petch and his crew, fifteen strong, raised the dust on Main Street as they thundered into town an hour after full light. Farrow, sweeping his store porch, had never seen so many armed riders on the street since the Civil War days. He ceased his sweeping to spare a thought for his two saviours. Up till now they had called all the tunes in their fight against Petch, but being realistic, and seeing the small army Petch had brought with him, he thought that the two wild *hombres*' hurtin-Petch days were over.

The riders drew up their mounts outside the cat house, but only Petch dismounted. With his face as hard-lined as an Apache bronco's about to ride out on a hair-lifting raid, he glanced at the blackened ruins that had been his saloon. Then, muttering curses, he stormed into the cat house.

Elizabeta met him in the lounge doorway. She had not seen to her hair or put on any make-up, wanting to appear as though still suffering from shock and fear at being threatened with harm, or worse, from a notorious outlaw. She had taken to heart what Mr Bodine had told her, that the man she slept with, and who gave her expensive gifts, had once robbed banks. And now she could see for herself that Bodine had spoken the truth about Pearson, or Petch, as he had called him. She had never seen such a cruel, mean-eyed glare in the eyes of a businessman before. She was having no doubts that he had made his riches by his gun. He scared her every bit as Bodine had at first, only more so, for she knew with sickening realization that if Pearson discovered that she was aware of his past her good days with him would be over and, more frightening for her, he would kill her to ensure that she didn't pass on the information that would finish his political ambitions in the territory. She would have to do some more acting.

'Oh, Jackson!' she cried, and with her eyes damp with forced tears she ran over to him and flung her arms around his neck and held him tight.

'The pig threatened to pistol whip me if I didn't give him the key to the safe!' she sobbed. 'And he told me that his partner was going to burn down this place. But it didn't happen; they must have got scared off!'

'Yeah, yeah, it's OK,' Petch said, pushing Elizabeta away from him. He had other things chewing away at him. 'Did the Mexican say anything about me?'

Elizabeta's look of surprise was genuine. 'But it wasn't a Mexican who robbed the safe, Jackson,' she replied. 'He was a Texan, a tall man. And he didn't mention you at all,' she lied. 'But according to one of the saloon's barkeeps it was a Mexican, a short, broad-shouldered *hombre*, who started the fire there.'

Petch rocked back on his heels as though buffeted by an invisible wind and Elizabeta saw his face slacken and drain of blood. For a moment or two she thought that he was going to suffer some sort of seizure. In those few moments Petch's mind had gone back to the night at Sawmill Creek — the night he had thought he had killed Raynor and Santos. Then he got a grip on his nerves; he now knew who his enemies were. And Raynor and Santos as good as they were, were only two men. The number of guns he had riding with him would make certain that his two old gang members died this time for real. Without saying another word to Elizabeta, he stamped out of the cat house, and saw that Rinegold and his two men had joined his crew.

'We'd like to ride with you, Mr Pearson,' Rinegold said. 'What you intend doin' is our business now. Those fellas who have been hittin' you, Mr Pearson, are the same fellas who shot down my boys in Sonora. We'd kinda like to get even with them.'

'You and your two men are welcome to ride with us, Mr Ringegold,' Petch replied. 'We're goin' to hit that Mex sheepherders camp hard. M'be threaten to hang one of them unless they tell where those bastards are.' He swung up into his saddle.

Before he gave the order to ride out, Ringegold, close-eying him, said, 'Do you know how many of them we're facin'?'

'Two men,' Petch said. 'A Texan named Raynor and Santos, his Mex pard. They were once business associates of mine, but a deal I did didn't sit well with them. They reckon I owe them money and they're causin' me all this trouble to get it back.' He raised his voice, 'OK, men let's move out!'

Ringegold and his two men swung on the rear of the column, Ringegold thinking that Raynor and Santos, Pearson's 'business' associates, wouldn't have sat on the board of the silver mine he was supposed to have owned. His owlhoot's nose smelt a double-cross by Pearson over some deal the trio had agreed to, like a bank robbery or some suchlike quick money-raising scheme. Not that it mattered, he had his own good reasons for shooting down Mr Pearson's former 'business' partners.

★　★　★

Lassiter had counted the riders splashing their way across the ford. It seemed that Petch had had enough of being poked in the eye with a sharp stick and had declared outright war against his tormentors. It was going to be a bad time for Raynor and Santos. If they wanted to stay alive they would be wise to forget their vendetta against the man who had tried to kill them and to ride south, back to Sonora. And to leave Mr 'Pearson' to reign as the big man in the territory.

Suddenly his black feelings began to lift as he thought of a wild-ass scheme, though no more crazy than the ones

Raynor and Santos had been pulling off, successfully. He grinned. '*Señora!*' he called over his shoulder, 'I'd be obliged if you could hitch the horse to the buggy, as soon as you can!'

He struggled up on to his feet and made his painful way to his room. He laid his canes up against his desk and sat down. Opening the top drawer he took out a Walker Colt and a box of shells and loaded the pistol then stuck it into the top of his pants. He hesitated for a moment before deciding to put the box of reloads back in the drawer, then closed it. One shot, if he was lucky, two, would be all he had time to do what he had to do. Before he could pull off a third shot he'd be dead.

17

'Why, the camp's deserted, boss!' Newton cried out as the XL crew halted their horses overlooking the sheepherders' camp. 'They musta got wind of us comin'!'

With an angry-eyed disappointed gaze, Petch took in the abandoned huts, the wind flapping tarp tents and the earth-blackened spots where the camp-fires had been.

'The sheep-stinkin' sonsuvbitches can't be far away,' he replied to his straw boss. 'Sheep can't be driven as fast as a herd of longhorns.' He nodded to the long ridge of mountains ahead of them. 'M'be only as far as those peaks. But before we pick up their trail we'll stomp this camp into the ground.'

★ ★ ★

Raynor looked along the smoking and chatting line of riflemen sitting with their backs up against the rock barrier blocking the mouth of the canyon. He had handed out the Winchester repeating rifles and pistols taken from the men he and Santos had killed to the elderly *hombres* who, Santos told him, had once been soldiers in the Mexican army. The boys were armed with the old battered stocks, single-shot rifles the sheepherders possessed to keep off the sharp-toothed predators.

They didn't have the look of a line of regimental sharpshooters, he thought, but by the grim set of their jaws, even the *chicos* would hold under fire. With the help of him and Santos, at the other end of the line, and their long held hatred for the Yankees, Petch and his roughnecks were in for one hell of a hot reception when they showed up.

★ ★ ★

Petch held up his right hand and the column halted. 'They must he bedded down in that draw,' he said, pointing to a narrow cleft in the rock face. 'The sheep have left a stinkin' trail a blind man could follow with his nose. We'll go in shootin' and a'hollerin', scare the livin' daylights out of those greasers, until one of them tells us where those two fellas we're after are lyin' low!'

'Don't you think we oughta go in on foot, army skirmisher like, Mr Pearson?' Ringold said. 'The way into that valley ain't all that wide; ridin' in will have us all bunched up makin' us easy targets.'

Petch swung round in his saddle and gave Ringold a sneering glare. 'You ain't scared of a bunch of Mex woollie men, are you? They'll only have a few old varmint-killin' rifles between them with hardly the cash to buy reloads for them. They'll run like frightened jack-rabbits when we burst in on them.' Petch's only worry was about Raynor and Santos's guns, but he opined that the pair would not be so foolish as to box themselves in a canyon with a bunch of spineless sheepherders.

Ringegold pulled his horse round and rode back the few yards to Slattery and Benteen.

'Boys,' he said, low-voiced, 'Pearson and his 'glory boy' charge could get us all killed. He's m'be right about those Mexes only havin' a few old rifles between them, but he's forgettin' that when those two lots of dead men came into town, their rifles, pistols and reload belts were gone. Now I've worked myself into a sweat wonderin' where all those guns have got to. The answer I'm gettin' back don't please me at all. I reckon the first of Pearson's men who reach the mouth of that canyon are goin' to find out where they are in the short time it takes them to die. So keep well back until we see how things play out.'

Petch drew out his pistol and fired a shot in the general direction of the canyon. 'Let's go and raise hell, boys!' he shouted and raked his horse's ribs with his spurs, sending it forward in a neck-straining gallop.

'Here they come, *hombres*!' Raynor said. 'Get to your firing positions!' He levered a shell into the chamber of the Spencer and rested it easily against his shoulder across the top of the sheltering rock as all the firing line turned and faced the oncoming enemy.

'Do not fire at the gringo dogs yet, *mi muchachos*!' Santos warned. 'Wait for my order. We want every shot to kill!'

Santos managed to hold back the tensed-nerved sheepherders until the charging riders were within rifle range then he yelled out the order to fire.

The volley came as a stick rattling along a railed fence rather than in one single ear-blasting roar, but it was just as effective, and Rinegold's fears were justified. The hail of lead cleared six men off their saddles and brought down three kicking and pain-squealing horses in a wild mêlée of curses and yells, stopping the charge in a dust-raising halt. Petch, and the surviving riders, withdrew under the screening dust cloud to the shelter of a dry wash that snaked its way across the flat behind them, though not before another three men fell victim to the deadly fire. Dismounting on the bed of the wash they climbed back up to the rim to give covering fire for any of the wounded to come on in. Not one of the crumpled bundles of men so much as stirred.

Ringold, lying close to Petch, had the sense not to give him a 'told you so' look. By his mad-eyed visage he reckoned that the rancher wasn't in the mood to be told he'd made a deadly blunder of things.

Petch was doing a lot of dirty-mouthing. He had miscalculated. Raynor and Santos *were* with the sheepherders. The Mexicans going into the canyon hadn't been a frightened, panic-stricken move, but a carefully thought out plan by the pair, a trap for him to ride into, and with his eyes open. Petch did some more cursing.

The sons-of-bitches had won every move they had made against him. Now it was time he came up with a tactic of his own that would see Raynor and Santos with their backs pinned up against a very hard wall. He twisted round and faced Rinegold.

'You, and your boys,' he said. 'sneak along this wash and where it bends round that juttin' out butte you can see a gully that runs right up to the rim line. If you keep low you can make it to the foot of the gully without those bastards in the canyon spotting you. It looks an easy climb up on to the ridge. Once there we'll have them between us.'

Rinegold gave Petch's plan a few minutes' thought. It could work. Three rifles firing down on them would have more than a line of Mexican *pacificos* cracking.

He glanced along at Slattery and Benteen. 'Let's do it, boys,' he said. 'But move slow and low, OK?'

Although it was only spasmodic rifle

fire coming from the wash it still could maim and kill and Raynor and Santos had to impress the jubilant Mexicans to keep behind the sheltering rocks, and that although they had won the first battle against the gringos, the small war wasn't over yet. Petch, Raynor and Santos knew, was an unforgiving man even on a good day, and this hadn't been a happy day for him. He had lost men, lost face, and he would be thinking hard of how he could get the edge on them and do some killing of his own. Raynor suddenly felt a chilling sensation between his shoulder-blades as he thought of how he would play things if he was in Petch's situation. He glanced up at the rock behind him.

'*Amigo*!' he shouted across at Santos. 'The sonuvabitch will be thinkin' of how he can outflank us by way of that wash. I'd be obliged if you could get up on that ridge behind me to see if I'm thinkin' right, or worryin' for damn all like some old maid.'

The three would-be outflankers,

sweating and panting, made it to the ridge without drawing any fire on themselves from the sheepherders. Slattery and Benteen slipped out of the gully, Ringold held back following them after a few moments while he removed a stone from his boot. It would only take Ringold that few seconds to find out that the stone in his boot had saved his life, and ended his run of luck.

'Jesus Christ!' Benteen gasped as a squat built Mexican rose out of the brush in front of him and Slattery. Both of them tried frantically to bring their rifles into play, too late by a lifetime.

Santos fired both of his pistols as fast as he could thumb back the hammers. The rapid discharges punched several killing shots into Slattery and Benteen, folding them at the kness as they dropped to the ground. Ringold, only part clear of the gully and partly shielded by Slattery and Benteen's falling bodies, felt the deadly heat of the shells as they hissed close by his face.

With life-preserving speed he flung himself back into the gully. Rolling, belly sliding, bringing an avalanche of stones and rocks with him, he tumbled down on to the bed of the wash. He struggled up on to legs that were as unsteady as a town's drunk's to find that along with his numerous cuts and scrapes he had suffered a shot in his right shoulder.

Petch heard the quick firing pistol shots, and started up with his cursing again. Raynor and Santos had sprung another successful trap. Then a bloodied-faced, dust-shrouded Ringegold came limping towards him.

Ringegold cold-eyed Petch. 'We met up with that Mex of yours on that ridge. He wasn't as tall as I've been led to believe, but he was tall enough to do for Slattery and Benteen. And it's only by a miracle the quick shootin' bastard didn't put me down for keeps. I fancy myself as a hard man, and rode with suchlike men, but the two broncos you're after are *hombres* you, and the boys you've still got with you, won't get the better of. I'm quittin' and headin' back to Tombstone. I've fairer chance of stayin' alive mixin' it with the Earps!'

He brushed past his former boss to make for his horse, thinking morosely that if he had paid heed to Slattery back there in Gila Crossing, he would still have a gang.

Petch didn't tell Ringold that he now knew that there had never been a 'tall Mexican'. It had been Raynor wearing Mex clothes who had fooled them all. He had been wasting time hunting for a man who never existed, allowing him and Santos to hit him at their own choosing. Petch was that angry with being so easily tricked and losing so many men for no gain, he was almost mad enough to back shoot Ringegold — a man he had paid good money to for the hire of his gun.

In his old bank-robbing days he would have gunned down any gang member who'd had a disgreement with him, fast. The loyalty of the six men he had left, after they had seen their buddies killed through his misreading of the situation, couldn't be depended on. Shooting Ringold in a mad-ass temper would have his crew turning against him. They could pull out leaving him to face the blood-hunters, Raynor and Santos, on his own, which meant signing his own death warrant. Then he would have to do some quitting of his own, like forgetting his grand ambition to become the big man in the territory and grabbing what cash and other valuables he had locked up in the ranch safe and heading west, to California, fast.

Though Petch's pressing worry was that he had lost control of the situation, there was no way now he and his crew could ride into the canyon to raise hell. They were pinned down in the wash until Raynor made his next move, then hope he could counter it with a quick thought-up tactic of his own.

Raynor was also racking his brain to come up with a plan to break the standoff. Santos had come down from the high ground with the good news that Petch had lost another two of his men, though growling angrily that he had failed to kill the third gringo. Then came a shout from one of the lookouts that a gringo was riding back to Gila Crossing.

'That means Petch has only about half the crew he came bold-ass ridin' in with, Santos,' Raynor said. 'It could be the time to take the fight to them. The sheepherders and their families can't stay undercover forever. Petch can head back to his ranch, leavin' a couple of riflemen in that wash to pick off any Mexican, man, woman or child, who shows themselves carelessly. We can't let that happen. We're beholden to them for helpin' us out and to make sure they don't pay for that help with their lives.'

Raynor remained silent for a few minutes, thinking hard. Then he smiled at Santos. 'We could go at Petch, Texas style, *amigo*.'

Santos favoured him with a puzzled scowling look.

'In the old Texan range-war days,' Raynor continued, 'when a rancher had some big disagreement over water or grazing rights with some poor sod-buster, one dark night his herd of longhorns would accidentally stam-pede, right across the sodbusters' growin' land. Flatten all the standin' corn or whatever, and m'be any outbuildin's in their path. While we ain't got a herd of cows to stampede there's a lot of sheep to hand. Those woollies ain't so heavy footed as longhorns, such as bein' able to turn barns into a heap of kindlin', but if they can be driven with some haste down into that wash they could spook Petch's boys' horses.' Raynor grinned. 'Now separate a cow hand from his horse and he's a lost soul. He'll not have the stomach to stay and fight off six or seven riflemen comin' in on him under all that dust the sheep will raise, he'll hare after his runaway horse.'

Raynor gave his plan another few minutes of screwed-up-face thinking before saying, 'What's got me beat is how the hell do we get those woollies up and wild runnin', bein' they're not so tetchy tempered as longhorns? We can't light a fire behind their asses in case we burn out the whole valley. And if we start shootin' over their heads it will alert Petch that we're plannin' something.'

'We only know how to rob banks and stages, *amigo*,' Santos said. 'But the camp *jefe* should know how to make sheep stampede. I'll go and ask him.'

Ten minutes or so later, a smiling Santos rejoined Raynor. It must be great news Raynor thought. Smiling was something his partner rarely did.

'Wolves,' Santos said. 'They'll send the sheep running. Wolves and coyotes are the animals' biggest fears. If they smell them or even hear those flesh eaters howl they'll take off as quick as any herd of spooked cattle.'

Raynor started to wonder if there

were any wolves and coyotes roaming around the canyon. If there were they must have smelt the presence of their greatest enemy, man, and cleared out of the canyon.

Santos's grin, on seeing Raynor's puzzled look, widened a fraction. 'We don't need real wolves, Juan,' he said. 'The *muchachos* will imitate wolves' cries.'

'Let's try it, Santos,' Raynor said, though not fully convinced the mock howls would work. 'I can't come up with a better plan. You organize six or so riflemen, I'll have some of those boulders moved aside, to allow the sheep free passage.' He grinned. I'll have to watch I don't get stomped on.'

* * *

'What the hell!' gasped a ranch hand as a great white mass of loudly bleating sheep came boiling out of the mouth of the canyon. He raised himself higher above the rim of the wash to get a clearer look at the oncoming herd then suddenly slid back down again, rifle dropping from lifeless hands, killed by a rifle shot none of the men in the wash had heard.

Petch lost control of his men. The XL crew had thought it would be an easy ride through a camp frightening the crap out of a bunch of greaser sheepherders but it had turned out to be a killing ground, for them. They had lost well over half of the boys and not so much as shot a sheep and now in a minute or two they'd be dodging woollies to stop themselves being knocked off their feet, making them easy targets for the Mexican sharp-shooters, who had just proved how sharp they were. They broke and slid down the sides of the wash to their horses, before the first of the sheep came tumbling over the rim. Petch saw them go, along with his grand future in Arizona. It was heading for California time with what he had in his safe. He would never make it as big again, but it was a longways better alternative than being dead. Which he would be if Raynor and Santos caught up with him. He ran to his horse, cursing his luck.

There was a general cheering and much back slapping among the riflemen as they saw the gringos cutting and running for it. Raynor and Santos strode around doing some congratulating of their own, and praising the *jefe* for the bravery of his men standing up against better armed men.

'My advice, *señor*,' Raynor said, 'once you have rounded up the sheep, is to head back to Mexico. It will not be long before Yankee lawmen call on you and start askin' you awkward questions. They'll not be happy at Mexicans shootin' down gringos even if in self-defence. I'm sorry me and Santos can't help you to rope in your sheep but our business with the *jefe* of the men you drove off is not yet finished and I fear that if we do not catch up with him he'll escape us again.'

'We were going back to Sonora,

amigo,' the *jefe* replied, 'the grass here is finished. Do not worry about the sheep; they are running south and once they reach their old grazing grounds in Mexico they'll stop running and we will catch up with them.' The old man's wrinkled face cracked in a grin. 'You and your *amigo*, the fearsome' *bandido*, José Santos, go and do your killing. My *muchachos* will bury the gringo dead. We will take their horses and guns as payment for the hard work digging the graves will cause us.'

After the last handshake and the final, '*Muchas gracias, amigos,*' Raynor and Santos got astride their mounts.

'We'll have to make ground up, José,' Raynor said. 'Petch knows that he's lost out and he'll only stop long enough at his ranch house to grab what he's got stashed in his safe and head for God knows where. And we can't expect another owlhoot drifter to come along again and tell me he bumped into my old gang boss in California, Nevada, or wherever.'

'We will take this trail,' Santos said, pulling his horse's head round. 'It is a shorter way through the canyon below where the sheep were. Once clear of the canyon we will be riding close to Petch's trail dust.

'Let us go then, *amigo*,' replied Raynor, digging his heels into his mount's flanks. 'Petch is long past due for bein' planted.'

18

Lassiter, standing at one of the windows of the ranch house counted the riders coming up the main trail to the house. His top lip curled back in a mirthless smile. Petch had returned with only five men. The big Texan and his Mex partner must have laid on a real hot reception for Petch and his crew. He hobbled across to Petch's desk and sat down in his big chair then picked up the Colt pistol from the desk and thumbed the hammer back to full cock and waited for the man he intended to kill to walk into the room.

As Lassiter had expected, he'd had no difficulty driving his buggy right up to Petch's big house; no ranch hand had stopped him to ask his business on the XL range. By his reckoning of the men Petch had led across the wash earlier on in the day, there couldn't be more than three or four men left at the ranch to keep a check on the cattle, a long way from the ranch house.

Petch's Chinese cook and houseman came out of the house on hearing the click-clack of Lassiter's support canes as he walked across the porch. Lassiter stopped and transferred his right stick into his left hand then his free one gripped the butt of the pistol sheathed in a shoulder holster under his left armpit.

Fierce-eying the cook, he said, 'I don't know if you savvy American, Chinese man, but if you don't step out of my way and go about your business, I'll plug your yellow hide.'

Whichever it was, the threatening pistol, the threatening voice, Lassiter didn't know, but with much high-pitched muttering in his own tongue the cook scuttled back into the house. Lassiter heard the sound of his slippered feet running towards the rear of the building.

Lassiter made his way along the

broad, carpeted passage opening every door until he found the room he was looking for: Petch's den. Rummaging in the top drawer of the dark oak desk he discovered the keys of the big safe standing in one corner of the room. Lassiter thin-smiled. He had hit the jackpot first time. Again freeing his hand of one of the sticks, he reached down and opened the safe and laid its contents down on the desk, three or four legal documents, wax sealed, and several neatly tied bundles of dollar bills, enough by a rough thumb count to meet the pay of the crew of the XL several years ahead.

Tired with all the exertion, Lassiter sat down at the desk and poured himself out a glass of Petch's whiskey from the bottle on the desk, to ease his pain while he waited for the rancher's return. Unless, he thought, Raynor and Santos had pulled off a miracle and disappointed him by shooting the son-of-a-bitch dead.

Petch and the remainder of his crew

came in riding rein-lashed horses, Petch making straight for the house, Newton and the ranch hands cutting off towards the bunk house, the straw boss still shaken by the shooting down of his men. He had never seen so many men killed before in so short a time since his war days. He was having an uncomfortable feeling that the pair who had set up the killing ground were not far behind them. And that their bloody mayhem was not over yet until they had gunned down his boss, which gave him strong thoughts about the wisdom of staying on as straw boss of the XL.

Petch quickly dismounted, not bothering to tie up his horse. He gave a cursory glance at the buggy and wondered why P.T. Sutton was calling on him. His dealings with the town's shyster were over. He pushed open the door of his den and stopped abruptly in the doorway. With the fleeting, but missing nothing look he used when assessing the potential hazards inside a bank he was about to rob, Petch took in the situation in his den. The crippled dude, armed up, sitting at his desk, and his getaway money lying in front of him. With an angry snarl, he clawed for his pistol.

The speed with which Petch had reacted on seeing him, almost caught Lassiter short. He had expected to get the drop on Petch and have a few minutes' gloating on how he'd turned the tables on the rancher before shooting him. Both pistols firing sounded as one discharge. Lassiter gasped with pain as he felt a hammer-like blow on his chest. The force of the point-blank shot rammed him hard against the back of the chair, overturning it on to the floor with his legs tangled around it. Then he passed out.

Petch clapped both hands to his middle, his face a grey mask of agony. Though he could see that his wound wasn't bleeding much, he had taken a bad shot; he was bleeding inside. A belly wound, if not treated urgently and expertly, was the road to a slow and painful death. All thoughts of taking the money from his desk were gone; his only priority was to get to his horse and somehow haul himself into the saddle and stay conscious on the ride to the sawbones in Gila Crossing.

His wound's fiery pain flared across his groin and into his hips stiffening up his leg movements making his progress along the passage like some tangle-footed drunk's walk.

Newton heard the shots and came rushing out of the bunk house and saw his boss come stumbling out on to the porch and made for him. He stopped his running as he heard the sound of hard-driven horses and whirled round, seeing for the first time the two expert killing men. Loyalty to the man who paid his wages caused Newton to make the decision not to quit the ranch but to make a fight of it: he stood with a pistol in his hand and faced the oncoming riders.

Santos rode straight at the armed gringo. Newton only had time to fire off one wild shot, no time at all to regret his rash decision to stay. Santos cut him down with a fusillade of shots, dead before he was flung to the ground. Santos pulled up his horse outside the bunk house, hawk-eying the door and the only window facing him.

'Hey, gringos!' he yelled. 'Are you going to be as foolish as your *compadre* lying out here? Or do you wish to stay alive?'

'We want no trouble, Mex!' a voice called out from the bunk house. 'You and your pard can do what you came here to do; we ain't goin' to stand in your way, honest!'

'*Bueno!*' replied Santos. 'But do not break your word or I will kill all of you, honest!' He kneed his horse to ride across to Raynor.

Raynor had ridden right up to the house, pistol cocked and ready to fire. He was puzzled why Petch hadn't already cut loose at him with the pistol he held down by his right side. Fully alert he halted his horse and took a longer look at Petch and noticed that he was drawn-faced with his left hand across his stomach and seemed to be having difficulty in keeping his balance. Then Petch's strange stance clicked home.

'Well I'll be damned!' he said to Santos, as he came up alongside him. 'Some fella has already shot the sonuvabitch!'

Both of them dismounted, though still keeping their guns aimed at Petch. Experience had taught them that things should not to be taken as they looked, if you wanted to stay alive.

'You ain't lookin' so well, Petch,' Raynor said mockingly. 'Ain't that so, Juan? A gut shot ain't my choice of a wound if I was to get plugged.' His voice steeled over. 'If there was a crick nearby I'd sling you in it so you could get the feelin's me and Santos got that night at Sawmill Crick.'

Losing all he had schemed for over the years, plus the possibility that he could have been dealt a fatal wound, raised enough hatred against the two men who had sicced all this grief on him for Petch to attempt a last chance at fighting back. With the sweat of his agony beaded on his brow, he forced himself to swing up his gun arm, a gun that felt as heavy as a blacksmith's block.

Dispassionately Raynor fired off one load. Petch dropped his pistol and slumped back against the wall then slowly slid down to the floor of the porch, leaving a blood trail on the planking from the bone shattering exit wound at the back of his head.

'That was for old Jud, Petch,' he said. Raynor gazed all around him then looked at Santos. 'It seems that those *hombres* in the bunk house have taken heed of your warnin', *amigo*,' he said. 'So let's go inside and see who Petch's unwelcome visitor was, and collect up our due.'

All tensed up, and still fisting their pistols, they walked into the only room with its door wide open. The man who had shot Petch could take them for a couple of his ranch hands and do likewise to them. They had had to do a lot of killing to get within touching distance of what Petch owed them and they didn't want to lose it by acting carelessly. Their nerves unwound a little when they discovered the room was empty — empty till they heard a man groan. Their hands tightened on gun butts as they walked round either side of the desk and saw the crumpled body of Lassiter on the floor.

Raynor sheathed his pistol and dropped to the floor. A quick glance told him the seriousness of Lassiter's wound. 'He's taken a bad chest shot, Santos. It's a miracle he's still breathin'. He may be an Eastern dude, but he was tough enough to stand all the pain he must have suffered gettin' here let alone face a hardcase like Petch.'

'He was a real *hombre*,' replied Santos. Which was praise indeed Raynor thought. There were very few gringos the old *bandido* thought well of.

Lassiter suddenly opened his eyes and looked up at Raynor. 'I missed the sonuvabitch,' he croaked, out of a blood-flecked mouth. 'He was too fast for me.'

'No you didn't, *amigo*,' Raynor replied. 'You aimed true and killed him; he was only takin' some time to die. I kinda helped him to quicken up that process.'

Lassiter gave a painful shadow of a smile. 'It seems that I saved you boys a job then,' he said. His smile froze and the light faded from his eyes as his head fell against Raynor's arm.

Raynor got to his feet and nodded at the desk. 'Let's get all that money where it belongs, in our pockets, and ride outa here.' He close-eyed Santos. 'Then, *compadre*, we'll have to work out what we are goin' to do with it; we ain't goin' to blow it in whorin' and gamblin' — it's been too hard to come by. I suggest we buy a cattle spread in Chihuahua, where the *desperado* José Santos ain't been heard of, for I hate to admit it but my bank-robbin' days are over. If that's OK with you, *amigo*.'

Santos, for his pride's sake, didn't answer Raynor straight away. He made as though he was weighing up his *compadre*'s suggestion. In truth he had the same thoughts regarding their old profession as Raynor. Robbing banks meant hard riding and cold camps, hardships he couldn't take any more.

'OK, Juan,' he said. 'We will buy a *ranchero* in Chihuahua and live like Dons, sleeping on soft beds and eating food that is cooked for us.'

They quickly began to pocket the money. Raynor picked up one of the documents on the desk, broke the seal and read it.

'We'll swing by that sodbuster's place we called at comin' here, Santos,' he said. 'These are the ownership papers of his land.' He grinned. 'We can tell him that before he suddenly passed over, Petch got religion, and wanted him to have the papers. Now let's vamoose, I've done enough killin' this day.'

The ranch hands in the bunk house had had their fill of seeing their *compadres* killed and, as the one-time *mal hombres* rode out, the ranch had the deep silence of a long deserted camp.

THE END

We do hope that you have enjoyed reading this large print book.

Did you know that all of our titles are available for purchase?

We publish a wide range of high quality large print books including:
**Romances, Mysteries, Classics
General Fiction
Non Fiction and Westerns**

Special interest titles available in large print are:
**The Little Oxford Dictionary
Music Book, Song Book
Hymn Book, Service Book**

Also available from us courtesy of Oxford University Press:
**Young Readers' Dictionary
(large print edition)
Young Readers' Thesaurus
(large print edition)**

For further information or a free brochure, please contact us at:
**Ulverscroft Large Print Books Ltd.,
The Green, Bradgate Road, Anstey,
Leicester, LE7 7FU, England.
Tel:** (00 44) **0116 236 4325
Fax:** (00 44) **0116 234 0205**

Other titles in the
Linford Western Library:

HAL GRANT'S WAR

Elliot James

When Hal Grant's father was bushwhacked in the street, it was the opening shot of a range war. Wealthy ranchers were determined to rid Lundon County of its sharecroppers and sodbusters eking out an existence in the marginal lands. Hal should have sided with his fellow ranchers, but he did not believe in mob law. He was caught in the middle — and no one was allowed to sit on the fence in a conflagration that was consuming a county . . .

THEY CALLED HIM LIGHTNING

Mark Falcon

A blow to the head had caused him memory loss and temporary blindness. Was he Mike Clancey, the name inscribed on the pocket watch he carried? And the beautiful woman's picture on the inside of the watch — was she his wife? He needed answers. Known as Lightning for his gun skills, riding Thunder, a black gelding, with fair play and talent he would bring a tyrant to justice — but it was a dangerous trail he must follow.